AshFiera

Book One
An AshFieran Duet

K.L. ANDERSEN

Trigger Warnings

Please keep your mental health your #1 priority. Below are some trigger warnings incorporated into this book.

- Depictions of grief and loss
- Death
- Parental Death
- Vulgar Language
- Violence
- Kidnapping
- Hostage Situations
- Sexually Explicit Scenes

Acknowledgments

I can't begin to express how grateful I am for those in my life who have encouraged my writing journey. Every single one of you are amazing, and a blessing to have in my life. I would like to thank my Husband, for putting up with my spurts of random thoughts, and scenes I had to gush about in the moment. you are forever the best support a girl could ask for. To my Mom, for being my first reader, and giving me motivation to work on that next chapter just to satiate your need to know what happens next. I love you. To my lovely friends Anna and Kira, I am so lucky to have found both of you ladies since moving to my new home, with your constant love and support. You are both the best! To my beta readers, Kelly and Lou thank you for taking a chance on a brand new baby author, and reading my story, you two are the best. To my new Author friend CB Woods, thank you for reading my story and giving me so many pointers, you are amazing and I am grateful you reached out to me! Last but not least, my beautiful friend Alicia. Thank you so much for helping me polish my words and for being my writing buddy. And of course for all the inspirational music you have turned me onto.

Blurb

When a young woman, who grew up in a different realm than the one her human/witch mother did. Is being chased from her home after assassins hunt them down, kill her mom, and attempt to take her. She finds herself whisked away into a portal, after falling over the ledge of a waterfall. Landing her in the middle of a living room in the human realm, where she meets her Grandmother and Aunt. She begins to build a new life while dealing with grief when her Aunt suggests training with a friend. After weeks of making friends, her guy friends are hosting a boxing charity event where she meets a mysterious tall, dark, handsome male.

But this male isn't who he seems when she runs into him again, outside her home in the woods, after another encounter with the assassins who find her human home. She flees with the mystery male when a family friend from her past finds her and reveals her mother has kept several secrets. She must uncover those secrets, leading her to the person responsible for sending the assassins.

Will she be able to go through with her revenge when she discovers who is behind it? And will she be able to keep those she loves safe?

To all my little book goblins who gobble up books about Magic, Dragon Pets, No-Entirely-Human Mates, Sex and like being called a Good Girl.
Well...
You're a VERY Good Girl.

Prologue
Raine

F ive Years Prior

Wiping the sweat slowly dripping down my temple, I stopped briefly, catching my breath, staring out across the field of tall reddish grass toward the creature, an Ashix, perched on top of a large gray, moss-covered boulder sitting outside the lush forests of Giant Sequoias. It was the place they called home.

This specific beast constantly watched my father, and I practiced our fighting skills outside our dwelling in those same fields. Often, my stomach would churn under the creature's unsettling gaze, waiting for her aggressive nature to rear its ugly head. To strike us where we stood.

The females had the worst tempers, as exemplified by this one, with her long, red-tipped claws, pearlescent scales, and a long tail. They may be dangerous, but I would stop and stare in awe at their marvelous beauty. The males showed off the brightest colors of blues, greens, and reds in hopes of gaining the attention of a life-mate in the more neutral-colored females.

My mother told me they were similar to the mythical

dragons found in fairy tales for children back in her home realm, where humans lived. However, she had described them as smaller than the ones depicted and slightly larger than a horse. But, no matter their size, they were still fiercely mannered and feared by the people of AshFiera.

When my mother first came to the Shadow Realm, she hid inside an old tree lying on its side deep in the forest. Staying rooted for several days, unwilling to come out after spotting a young Ashix outside the waterfall closest to our home. It was quite a shock to her. Of course, that was until my father found and saved her, claiming her as his mate.

And every day, the female Ashix, whom I had taken to naming Beauty, was always watching, waiting for something to happen before making her move. So, we were always vigilant when we noticed her perched on top of that same boulder.

Today, my father tasked me to spar with him after my morning warm-up using the long sticks. These were long, cylindrical poles that needed to be handled with both hands, precisely. If hit with one, the bite of the impact stung as a reminder to pay attention. Luckily, Beauty wasn't on her boulder, keeping guard today.

A sigh left me at the relief coursing through my body. My father could be brutal with his hits if I didn't watch him closely. And I would rather Beauty not be here if that were the case today. When his brutal hits would land, he told me it would help build my pain tolerance, which could be helpful one day. I rolled my eyes at that, behind his back, of course. I would never let him catch me doing it to his face. The consequences were severe and often left lasting bruises.

"Raine, step to the left quickly and thrust your arm at

me," my father instructed. I did as he asked, but apparently, it wasn't quite what he needed.

"Faster! You need to learn to utilize the gifts I know you received from me to pick up your pace. Otherwise, you *will* fail against any of your enemies because no doubt they will be faster than you."

I was sure I could be faster, but I was sluggish today, likely due to the running we did yesterday to the little village nestled several miles away. He knew I had limits to how much I could do. I'm still half-human, and yesterday, he pushed me too far. I wasn't sure why, but suddenly, he was trying my patience. He never used to, but I gritted my teeth in anger at him. "Father, you know I'm tired today. We did so much yesterday. I need a break."

He snorted at my defiance, "My little Ashix, I push you only for your benefit. You will thank me later when that extra stamina and strength come in handy."

I despised the grin he gave me and, at that moment, the nickname he blessed or cursed me with a while ago when I had my first angry outburst. I still debated which one it was every other day. It made my anger start to simmer back up again. I grabbed one of the long sticks and threw the other to my father, readying myself for a fight. Back and forth, our sticks clashed. *SMACK, SMACK, SMACK.* Thunder boomed every time they made contact. The vibrations running up my arms bordered on painful stinging. I knew I needed to back off soon. My energy and anger were already draining, but all too fast; Father hit my arm before that happened. I didn't block him hastily enough. A scream left my throat from the burning pain. Then, hissing and growling came from deep in the woods, echoing around us as they rushed closer at an alarming speed.

Father stepped in front of me, readying himself for a

fight and blocking my view of what charged toward us from the forest. I didn't need to see what came toward us because I knew. "Beauty," I whispered.

Peeking out from the side of my father, I needed to gauge how close she was.

Charging through the tall grass, Beauty let the smoke billow out of her nostrils, her mouth wide open in a sinister, animalistic grin, revealing her many sharp teeth and angry, burnt orange eyes locked onto my father.

I needed to stop her before she could hurt him or, in return, get hurt herself.

Stepping out to the side of my Father, I moved forward. Holding my hand up, shaking, I screamed, "Stop!" Tiny bolts of purple shot out while I felt faint buzzing at the tips that faded swiftly. The brief confusion passed through my body, and I shook my head, refocusing on the Ashix.

She had skidded to a stop inches from my raised hand. The beast sniffed the air, looking me up and down from head to toe. My eyes widened in terror while my heart wildly pounded as I stood frozen. She had never come this close to us before; she always kept her distance.

So, I spoke softly to her. "Hey, sweet girl, I'm okay. He's not hurting me."

The Ashix stood looking back and forth, her gaze landing on Father again, narrowing.

I tried again to keep her attention focused on me, "Shh, it's okay, Beauty. I can handle myself against him. You don't need to worry."

The deadly Ashix bore her gaze into me, further leaving us at a standstill, staring at each other. My father shifted himself behind my back, causing Beauty's gaze to dart his way, huffing out another small trundle of smoke in his direction. It was almost like she could understand what I was telling her. And after a very long standoff, she turned around, swishing her tail, while leisurely walking back through the grass field. She jumped back up to her spot on the boulder, laying her head down while those burnt orange eyes stayed focused solely on me.

"Looks like Raine has a new friend, Lazarus. You will need to be more careful during training now if the beast sticks around, as the female has decided to claim our daughter," chuckled my mother, who was kneeling over one of her plants in the garden, looking over at us.

Peering at my mother, I smiled. She was so beautiful, sitting surrounded by greenery as the sunlight hit her curly, dark chocolate hair just right, making the warm, honey highlights adorning it glow brightly. Her emerald-green eyes sparkled as she stared at me, her full lips spreading into a sly grin. Some of my parents' closest friends would say I was a spitting image of her, a mini twin they called me. And since my mother was an actual twin, they had always laughed it off as a joke, but secretly, I loved looking exactly like her.

"You have been blessed by the Goddess, Raine. Being claimed and protected by them is a gift." A small tear escaped her eyes as she whispered to me.

Father, interrupting our heartfelt moment, murmured, "Come, little Ashix, it's time you clean yourself up before dinner. You have done more than enough this evening."

My parents walked side by side toward our home while I trailed behind them at a distance. Before entering the house, I looked back over my shoulder to the boulder where Beauty still lounged and, when I found her, still stared at me. I swore her head dipped in a bow of respect while bringing her tail to curl around her body. Not wanting to be rude and unsure if I witnessed it correctly, I dipped my head the same way before turning back around and entering my home.

LATER THAT EVENING, while lying in bed gazing at the darkened ceiling, not able to sleep yet, I daydreamed about ways to sneak closer to Beauty again. Suddenly, a door slammed, and muffled voices came from downstairs.

Sliding out from under my sheets, I snuck toward my door, only opening it enough to let my small body sneak past. Any further, and the door would creak, giving away that I had left the comfort of my bed.

Tiptoeing down the hall, I made sure to avoid the loose floorboards. I knew which ones they were, as I had liked to creep out of my room to sit outside and admire the sky, dancing in purples, blues, and pinks most nights when I couldn't sleep. Mother called the lights an Aurora Borealis, something similar the sky did in her home realm, Earth. It was called something else here, but I could never remember. Instead, I appreciated the human name for it.

My mother and father stood in the foyer, speaking in hushed tones to one another to avoid waking me. What they didn't know was that I was already awake and listening to their conversation.

"Laz, you're going to leave in the middle of the night? Are you even going to say goodbye to Raine?"

"Pandora, my love, you are too soft on our daughter. She will be perfectly fine and will understand that we don't always need to bid someone farewell when they leave on a short trip."

Already, the agitation in his voice flickered as he spoke

to my mother. Whenever he would leave on one of his 'trips,' I was always there, ready to wave him off, no matter the time, day, or night.

What makes this night any different?

I loved him dearly, but I hated it when he had to leave, as we never knew when or if he would return. His profession as a Shadow Assassin was hazardous and always possessed the potential of never returning.

I scoffed at how he told her she was too soft on me. She certainly was not, especially when I would wreak havoc while he was away. Giving my poor mother more gray hairs than necessary.

"Lazarus, please, just go wake her up. It would crush her, and you know this." My mother's persistence upheld, pleading with him. I swallowed the lump in my throat, waiting for his next reply.

"I will not repeat myself. I am already running behind schedule." It was a final statement. He handed my mother a small wrapped box with a bow on it. "Here, give my little Ashix this when she wakes. Tell her always to wear it and remember that I will always come back home to my girls."

I sat stunned, unable to move.

Was my father leaving without saying a word to me?

My heart hammered violently in my chest as if trying to escape the cavity where it lay beneath. My Father's hand on the doorknob, ready to turn, paused. Turning his head slightly to the side but not looking up at me, he nodded, and out the door he left. It was his way of saying goodbye, and for tonight, it would have to do, but it still stung and hurt me deep down.

Several moments passed when my mother's soft voice called for me.

"Raine, come here, baby. I know you're awake."

My feet moved on their own down the wooden stairs, creaking along the way. My head bowed in submission as I thought I was in trouble for eavesdropping or maybe even for being out of bed. Making it down the last stair, I did a little hop off to the floor, looking at my mother innocently. I gave her a small smile, "Sorry, Mom. I know I'm not supposed to be out of bed. There was a bang that woke me up."

"Hush, it's alright. I'm not mad."

She sighed and brought forward the box that my father had handed her just before he left, instructing her to give it to me the next morning. But, instead, she presented it to me now.

"Your father left this for you. I'm sure he won't be gone long, though." She said, slightly wincing.

Barely catching the flinch, I wanted to ask if she was okay, but as I went to open my mouth, she placed the small box in my hands.

Forgetting the look, I smiled broadly. Looking down, my hands moved on their own, unwrapping the box. A sloppy bow, placed half haphazardly at the top, suggested that Father had most likely attempted to tie it himself.

I giggled to myself as I went to rip the bright red paper. Underneath was a black box. The top slid off easily, and inside, laid on silky, thin black fabric, was a beautiful locket and chain. Picking it up, I examined it, rubbing my thumb across the designs. The locket was layered with flames of different sizes along the edges, and in the center, engulfed in the fire, was an Ashix.

Wiping a tear from my cheek, I smiled softly. Looking up at my mother, rivets of tears fell silently from her eyes, and I hugged her tightly. "It's okay, Mom. I promise he will not be gone long. I know it."

With the locket held tightly to my chest, I hugged and kissed my mother goodnight, heading up the stairs in a rush to my bedroom.

Finally, in my bed again, I looked over the locket closer and opened it up. I didn't think anything was inside, as it was brand new, but then a small piece of paper fell onto my blanket. Examining it, I unfolded the paper, and it was a short note from my father:

To My Little Ashix,

May this locket always remind you that you are as fierce as the female Ashix, who now watches over you. I will be home soon.

Your Father

Lying down the note and locket on my bedside table, I lay my head on my silk pillow, thinking only of the love my father conveyed in his gifts, making me smile. Even if he never said the words out loud, he always made a point of showing instead of telling me. Yawning, I drifted off into the darkness of a dreamless sleep while the world around me kept turning.

Chapter One
Raine

Five years—five long years of not knowing what happened to my father. He left that night and never came back, even though he had promised to in the letter that sat atop my bedside table in a small wooden picture frame. That night was the first and last time he left without kissing me goodbye. I was just thirteen then.

And I hated him.

I hated how he evoked so many different emotions. The fickle guilt of not stopping him and demanding one last hug. Saddened by the many memories I could have had with him. He was not able to teach me more about life in AshFiera. Lastly, the anger, like the rage, was boiling in my blood, making my skin hot. And although I harbored all that anger, I still loved him with everything I had. I was his little girl, his shadow, his little Ashix. I aspired to grow up and emulate him, a renowned city Shadow Assassin who traveled the world, sometimes across realms, to help eliminate the evil lurking beneath the surface.

I needed to move on, though. There was no way he could be alive. I couldn't bring him back from the possible death I feared had happened to him, and instinctively, I knew something had happened. What that something was, my mother and I would never find out.

Ugh, it's time to get up for the day. The first thoughts of the morning trickled out as I could only ponder for so long before Mother barged in and urged me to get my lazy ass out of bed, *lest we waste the day away*, she would say.

Quickly, I dressed in a pair of tight black leggings, turning my body to admire the way they made my ass look, which was fantastic, while slipping on a plain white tank top that would keep me cool during my morning activities, and then pulling my long, wavy dark chocolate hair in a high pony to keep it from sticking to my neck when the inevitable sweat dripped from my hairline.

I was almost ready to head outside for my morning run, but I missed one thing. Scouring for my locket again, somehow I had misplaced the dang thing. But when my stomach growled and my short search turned up nothing, I stopped looking and urgently needed something to munch on before I headed out on my run. Leaving the comfort of my bedroom, I pushed the door open and walked down the creaky hallway toward the kitchen.

Before I could hit the bottom step, my mother was waiting for me by the front door of our foyer, eyes locked directly onto me.

"Hey, Mom, morning!"

Quirking her right eyebrow up, she eyed what I was wearing. "Raine, did you forget what today was?" She asked.

"Uhh, maybe?" I squeaked and gave her my best 'I'm innocent' smile to placate whatever I had forgotten.

"We are supposed to go together to the village and deliver these herbs to the healer as we do every week. We are getting low on several things I can not grow or make myself." She said, shifting to the side.

Her slender finger pointed at the large, long table by the door; four large, handled wicker baskets sat filled with various cleaned, edible, and medicinal herbs. Every week, she needed help carrying them. The more we brought at one time, the more likely we were to get our usual list of supplies. It took hours to walk to the small village and back, so it was dire that we left soon.

Mom and Uncle Cassius had explained to me when I was younger that AshFiera was less modernized than the light realm, Earth. For one, they had motorized vehicles, and we didn't, but that was more so because the only people who needed to travel far distances were the Shadow Assassins. They had other, more convenient abilities.

"Shoot, I totally didn't realize what today was. I was just about to run before hitting the bags," I said, but when I saw my mother's eyebrows shoot up further, if that was even possible, I redirected myself. "But I'm gonna go grab a bite, and then I will be ready to leave," I called over my shoulder, already on my way to the kitchen to grab some food that would silence my grumbling stomach.

Grabbing an apple and one of my mother's homemade oat bars, which she only made for me, using ingredients from her ever-expanding garden, I rounded the counter just as my mother's voice echoed from the front of the house.

"Hurry up there, we gotta get going, Raine," Mom said impatiently.

I understood the rush too well. We didn't want to be out after dark, especially if one of the many males inhabiting the village decided to bother Mom for a date or offer us an escort home in hopes of a hot meal.

She didn't date, though, not after my father's disappearance. I had always thought that maybe she was too heart-broken over him, or perhaps she just enjoyed being alone. I didn't know and didn't dare ask.

The only male who came around was Uncle Cassius, Mom's best friend and my trainer. He helped me practice defensive skills, so I wouldn't slack off and forget everything my father had taught me when I was younger. He made sure I used every tool available to defend myself and Mom in case things went south with anyone who wanted to take advantage of two females.

I rolled my eyes just thinking about the times he pretended I beat him to the ground just to elicit a smile on those hard days when I was missing Dad and acting out, making my mom's life difficult. He stood six feet five inches, towering over Mom and me, easily over our five feet three. He ribbed us at every opportunity, often calling us short stuff.

Shaking my head clear, I glided up to Mom with an oat bar stuffed into my mouth, chewing it fast so I could devour my juicy apple before leaving. Talking around a mouthful of food, I smiled, "Ready to roll."

Mom quirked an eyebrow up again, not saying a word. She grabbed two of the baskets, leaving the other two for me, and headed out the door towards the village of Martslocke.

Silence stretched between us for most of the walk until I couldn't take it anymore. Anxious energy burned inside waiting to be set free.

"So, are you finally going to accept one of the many callers when we arrive at the village, or will you sneer at them again?" I asked her with a side glance, trying to gauge her mood for the day.

She didn't answer me, though, and let out a long sigh,

indicating she wouldn't either. I didn't understand her reluctance to spend time with someone. I often wondered if I would catch the eye of a male in Martslocke someday. I was nearing nineteen and very much into males. I once tried to spark some flirting with one, but it seemed they were as reluctant as my mother to give me the time of day. So here I was, just like my mother, without a mate.

Finally, upon reaching the village, it seemed busier than it had ever been during past visits. It was so–lively. Children were running, laughing, and screaming as they chased each other around the large water fountain, which had been decorated with several Ashix spitting out water instead of fire.

The shop we needed to visit was conveniently located near the fountain, allowing us to move swiftly and avoid the crowd that gathered around a vast market. Several vendors were lined up outside in the middle pavilion, their stalls were laden with goods for selling, offering a variety of items, including food, clothing, weapons, and even a pet handler. The weapons stall piqued my interest as I watched the vendor show off a dagger to a customer. The glimmer of a new blade distracted my motion and drew me in.

"Mom, can we go over and check out some of the vendors before we leave? Please? Maybe if we have enough, I could procure a new weapon?" I tried giving her my best doe eyes while letting my eyelashes flutter for dramatic effect. It usually worked, as I found she couldn't say no to me very often. I think part of it was guilt that I didn't have my father around, and part of it was that I rarely asked for anything anyway.

"Maybe my little Ashix. We have a lot to carry home today." She said, not giving way to my tricks.

Giving her a slight pout, I shuffled my feet after her, but

then picked up the pace when she looked back over her shoulder. I swore her eyes had sparkled with purple lightning bolts, like she was giving a warning.

I knew she had powers and was known as a witch in the human realm. She never showed those powers to me, though, but I could decipher them in the earth when I was far from her or in the air after it had rained. I believed I had those same abilities, although mine radiated through my body in a different way. It was more intense when I could peek at it, but it was muted.

After my father's disappearance, I had a short spell where my anger was out of control. For several days, I kept blowing apart my homemade boxing bag with my fists alone. Mom would put it back together overnight every time it happened when I was sleeping, but after a week, she roped Uncle Cassius in to help me channel my anger elsewhere. I guessed she got tired of mending my broken bags.

Reaching the shop, The Healing Shadows, I must have been distracted, as Mom was already inside. I ran to catch up to her. Just then, I bumped into a male as he exited the shop. "Oof, sorry. I wasn't paying attention and didn't realize anyone was coming out the door."

He glared at me, at least with his right eye. His left was covered with a dark gray patch, a scar that started mid-eye and hooked around his cheekbone into the chestnut-colored hairline of his temple. He was attractive except for the sneer on his lips, showing off one of his sharp fangs. The stubble on his face told me he likely hadn't shaved in a few days, and it worked for him. Everything about him drew me in, but my instincts were blaring red lights screaming at me that he was dangerous. Like an Ashix for all that beauty on the outside, underneath the surface was a vicious streak readying for attack. And it was clear that he was unhappy I had accidentally bumped into him.

"Watch where you're walking, female, before you hurt yourself or run into the wrong sort." His voice was deep and growly, like that of the Metine, big, fluffy fuckers who had long claws, sharp teeth, and a scrunched-up nose. They usually left you alone and were not aggressive like the Ashix, but they still sounded scary as shit, especially in the dark when they blended in with the shadows.

I turned back to the male, who was being an obvious dick, "Look, I apologize. No need to be a growly asshole. If you'll excuse me, you are in my way of entering this shop." I swept my hand toward the building he blocked me from entering. The unknown male didn't like what I had to say when a snarl left his throat.

"Careful who you talk to like that, female. As I said, you never know how dangerous someone could be." His honey-speckled eye stayed attached to every move I made before I spoke while trying to brush past him into the shop.

"Pft, okay, Patches. Gotcha. I will take your advice, be careful, and don't talk to rude strangers." Strolling around his unmoving body, I rolled my eyes, which he couldn't see me doing, and went into the shop.

Well, that was weird.

Mom's lovely, feminine voice beckoned me toward the back of the long shop.

"Oh, perfect, there you are, Raine. What held you up? I thought you were right behind me?" She asked.

"Uh, Oh. You know, just running into strange dick-headed males on my way in and arguing with them." I said with a twinkle in my eyes, so she would think I was joking. Still, that encounter made me uneasy—something like anxious butterflies fluttering around in my stomach, thinking of the mysterious male. I had a bad vibe that radiated around him and hoped I would never run into him again. It would be a blessing from the goddess.

Mother leaned against the counter and held out her hands to me, silently asking me to hand over the baskets. "Sorry, Xidas. As I was saying, here are the remaining herbs you requested. I'm hoping this will be sufficient and allow us to obtain the things needed on the list I gave you the last time I was here."

The shopkeeper, Xidas, an older male with shocking white hair and even more shocking white eyes, which would have you think he was blind, but he certainly wasn't, glanced over all four baskets. "These are fantastic, Pandora. You truly are an Earth Goddess for how bountiful and big these herbs look."

Mom's cheeks turned pink at his praise.

"Yes," he continued, "these are perfect and much more than I expected. Here, there is some extra coin for you and Raine to use at the market if you so wish." He slid over a big bag of clinking coins. I looked wide-eyed at it and then at my mother, realizing there was more than enough to splurge on a few unnecessary items if we wanted.

Mom started to shake her head, but the old male held up his hand and said, "Please, Pandora. You always bring me the finest herbs, which seem to last longer than they should without even needing to be preserved. It's the least I can do to make up for the years of having the best."

"Thank you, Xidas, this is much appreciated!" Mom choked, wiping a stray tear that was trailing down her cheek.

I smiled at him, grateful for the kindness he always showed us. "That's incredibly kind of you, Xidas, thank you."

After finishing up our business, we left the shop and headed to the busy market. Walking around was a treat as the scents of different dishes made my mouth water. We had almost made it past the pet handler stall when I stopped briefly to scratch the underside of a cat's chin. I couldn't resist. They were just too adorable, with their large, round eyes and silky-soft fur. Usually, the village held weekly markets, but this week, the market day was switched to accommodate some important individuals arriving tomorrow to visit Martslocke. No one recalled who it was, but it sure was the talk of the village everywhere we went.

It was getting late, and we had to leave soon, so Mom directed us to the weapons vendor. I couldn't hide my excitement and immediately browsed, looking for the dagger I had seen earlier. It was a bland blade, but I had always wanted something small to carry with me, and I knew we may perhaps be able to afford it easily today with all the extra coins Xidas had given Mom.

I kept looking for that one weapon, but my eyes stopped suddenly on a different dagger. This was not the one I had browsed earlier. It had a beautifully designed black handle with swirls and flames entwined, which featured an iridescent blade. I had never regarded anything like it.

I looked over at Mom, who seemed distracted, looking around at the crowd.

"Hey, check this out, Mom. It's so beautiful, what do you think?" I asked, trying to shake her from whatever was worrying her.

And something was definitely distracting her when a few moments later, she finally responded, "Hmm, yes, it is stunning. Why don't we get it and then head home? It's starting to become late."

I nodded and got the attention of the weapons keeper,

pointing to the dagger. He grabbed it, and instead of wrapping the blade, he stuck it into a sheath and handed it to me. "Oh, I just wanted the dagger. I'm unsure· if we have enough for the sheath as well."

"Nonsense, young lady, this is on the house. Every dagger should have one. Now put the large strap around your waist, and the smaller one will go around your thigh." He had instructed as I reached for the new weapon, which felt heavy in my hands.

With the slight weight of my new dagger on my outer thigh, we set off through the village and back home.

As we reached the outer edge, an unknown male stepped out of the alley. He had a wide grin and sunken eyes set on my mom. "Hello, pretty females. May I escort you home? Perhaps you could show mercy and invite me in for dinner as a token of appreciation for safe travels? I haven't eaten anything in days," he said as he shifted from side to side, an action that caught my attention while nervous energy flowed through the air.

Looking further at him, I identified his pale, sickly skin. His greasy hair and the unwashed smell emanating from him indicated that he hadn't showered in days. I stepped in front of my mother, replying first, "No, thank you. We can manage on our own." Instinctively, I reached for my new dagger, unclasping the strap that held it in the sheath.

His gaze was drawn to my movements, and he frowned, but nodded and walked away quickly without another glance.

"What a weird day! That's the second male who has either bumped into me or just appeared that I have never seen before," I muttered under my breath to myself, but Mom caught every word.

She snapped her head over to look at me and asked,

"Another male spoke with you while we were here? What did he look like and say to you?" Her questions were rapid, and the worried lines that were etched on her forehead wrinkled further.

So I told her about the male I bumped into outside the shop we had visited. Leaving out a few physical details since I didn't want her to know, I found his bad-boy look appealing. When I finished, I realized it was an even weirder interaction now that I had said it out loud to her. If someone were to run into another person by accident, they would apologize and move along. At least the village's people were never aggressive, unlike the Shadow Assassins, who sometimes frequented villages on a job, but those AshFierans usually stayed in the big cities.

All the way home, Mom seemed more rigid and tense. When we finally arrived, Uncle Cassius was waiting for us near the garden, and Mom visibly relaxed. "Uncle Cass, what brings you to the neighborhood? You're a little far from home, don't you think?" I chuckled, knowing he did live far away but could shadow-jump to us in seconds.

Shadow-jumping, oh, how I wished that was one of the gifts my father had given me, but alas, it never showed itself.. When I was younger, he was disappointed that it had never manifested. Most of the time, someone who could shadow-jump was usually recruited to be a Shadow Assassin, hence the name.

I rolled my eyes, thinking about how 'super original' it was.

The gift enabled the person to teleport between locations in mere seconds. Usually, it only manifested in the male population, but occasionally, there were female shadow-jumpers. I had looked up to them and wanted to be like the females, for they had more strength than the males did in more than one way.

Dad introduced me to a female shadow-jumper once, and I was in awe of her, especially her confidence and the way she would make the males bend to her will with just one deadly look, almost hypnotizing them, but I figured they were scared of her power and strength.

"Kiddo," Uncle Cass said, snapping me out of my daydream. A low whistle blew through his lips while looking at my thigh. "That's a mighty pretty blade you have attached to yourself. What did you do, steal it from some poor soul in the village today?" He asked while chuckling and reaching for my hair to ruffle it. But I was too quick and stepped out of the way.

"No. Mom got some extra coins this trip and let me get a new weapon. Isn't she beautiful?" I said.

"Yeah, kid. She is a thing of beauty. Hey, why don't you go inside and clean up before dinner? I brought something special and need to have a little talk with your mom privately before eating." Uncle Cass said. My interest piqued at what he brought us to eat. Usually, it was something we normally wouldn't consume unless he procured it.

"Sure, see you guys in a few." I shrugged before heading for the door. I glanced at the boulder where Beauty usually rested. *Hmm, she still hasn't returned. Maybe I will catch her in the morning,* I thought while entering the house. It didn't surprise me she wasn't there, but a small voice deep down told me there was something off about her absence.

While inside, I decided to head to my room again to look for my locket. I still couldn't find it, and I swore I placed it on the second shelf of my bookcase next to a statue of an Ashix. The locket was the last gift my father gave me, and the only time I took it off was to shower or sleep. I always set it in the same spot every time so that I wouldn't lose it or break the precious memento. I needed to ask Mom if she had seen or moved it. It had been a few days without the pendant, and something inside me suffered its loss.

The noise of Mom and Uncle Cass entering the house disturbed my search, so I left my room to join them and eat whatever delicious dish he brought.

When I entered, I noticed they were both already sitting, so I decided to ask about the necklace before we ate, "Mom, have you seen my locket? It's been missing for a few days, and I thought I had placed it in my usual spot."

"No, baby. I haven't seen it, I'm sorry. We can look for it tomorrow after your morning run if you want. I do have to make sure the weeds are pulled in the garden before it gets too hot out," she said, glancing at Uncle Cass before digging back into her dinner.

I shrugged it off, nodding to her while scarfing my dinner quickly. It was getting late, and exhaustion set in from walking to the village and back home. I needed to head to bed so I might rise before the sun and do a longer run to make up for missing today. "I'm beat; it's been too long a day and I'm ready to turn in for the night. See you in the morning, Mom. Uncle Cass, I hope you will join me in a couple of days for our training." I said, leaving the table to bring my dirty dishes to the kitchen counter.

"Of course, night, kiddo," he said.

"Night, baby, I will see you in the morning." Mom blew a kiss as I left the room.

Walking up the stairs felt like an endless adventure, with my legs aching as I slowly trekked up. I showered in record time, which was a change from my usual routine of standing under the spray until Mom hollered at me to remove myself. Afterward, I put on my shorts and a thin, strapped tank before slipping under my slim summer blanket. I needed to sleep, but I lay there, silent in my sheets, staring at the dark shadows dancing across my ceiling, replaying the two strangers I had encountered that day.

The first male had to have been a Shadow Assassin. He wore the leathers and weaponry for one, and the eye patch didn't help him blend in much, either. The second male was not so unusual. It had happened before when my mother and I were in town. Some of the males were starving, likely from their inattentiveness to take care of themselves, always trying to convince us to let them walk us home, knowing damn well they would get fed.

Everyone knew who Mom was, even though she was a witch from the human realm. And father, being from AshFiera, was a well-known and feared male by most. But Mom was the exact opposite with her kind and caring soul. She took pity on those less fortunate, using her gifts to help soothe aches or bless the seeds people would bring her to sow on their own.

Thinking of my mother's kind heart, my eyes began to get heavy, and I couldn't resist letting myself dive back into my dreams that night, thinking about Beauty and Assassins and the dagger I was eager to practice with.

Chapter Two
Raine

The sun was barely peeking out from the horizon before I left the house to go on my run. I assumed Mom had been awake, probably lying in bed reading as she did every morning, but I still tried to remain quiet as I left.

Standing on our front deck, making sure my running shoe laces were tied tight, I readied myself, taking off in a run toward the woods where the Ashix resided. As I got older, I lost some of the fear I'd had as a child, thanks to Beauty's decision to protect our property and me. I didn't look for her on the boulder this morning, like yesterday, since I figured she wouldn't be awake yet. One thing was certain: her laziness; she never got up before the sun was completely over the horizon, shining bright and warming her favorite perch, the boulder.

It was quiet in the forest; of course, it would be. Everything was still sleeping, and it was just what I needed to calm my nerves from the day before. I still couldn't shake my intuition that something was off; it had been that way for a few days, something in the atmosphere had shifted the auras of the few people we encountered yesterday, even the wildlife and plants that resided here.

Mom once explained that I was in tune with others' feelings and more empathetic than most, so I experienced every slight shift, and at times, it affected me greatly.

The forest beyond was littered with Giant Sequoias that towered so high, it required you to crane your neck back to view the tops. Each tree grew trunks as large as five men standing side by side with arms stretched out wide, and as little as four men standing closely together. Some pines and ferns were scattered here and there, breaking up the scenery, but the ancient Sequoias dominated the space, making the sun's rays shine through their leaves like flashlight beams.

Mom and Uncle Cass taught me early on that most of AshFiera resembled Earth, hiding in the shadows of the other, much brighter world. Even with the travel arrangements so different, our world closely followed the humans.

It made me feel closer to Mom's home, though. I had wished we could visit her realm so I could meet my aunt and grandmother. When I was younger, she told me it wasn't possible, as my father had forbidden her from going back, and he wouldn't take her while he was still alive.

Although he had been away for several years, I still didn't understand why he hadn't allowed the travel, so I asked her again. She explained she couldn't remember the spell she had cast to gain access in the first place. It was hidden inside her family's ancestral spell book in the human world. Uncle Cass wasn't allowed to bring us either. As a Shadow Assassin himself, he took an oath in his younger years that forbade him from shadow-jumping with anyone other than another Shadow Assassin or one of his assignments.

By now, the sun had reached above the horizon just as I made my way to the Ashix Waterfalls. Most of the forest and nearby falls were named to honor the beasts; no one fought it. It was their home, after all, and the only place you would run into one of the beasts was if they were around. Most of the time, they were great at hiding, so it didn't surprise me that none were near as I approached the falls.

I took a deep breath, found a large rock to sit on, and overlooked the flowing water. The top of the falls stretched at least twelve feet higher than where I sat. I had found the best spot, overlooking the ledge that dropped another twenty feet into an underground lake. I never dared to jump off; clusters of sharp rocks were hidden underneath the water's surface. It was incredibly tempting, alluring.

When Beauty came with me on my late morning runs, I would admire her gliding from the top and disappearing further under the ground before the splash of her body connected to the surface and echoed.

Smiling softly, I lifted my face to a sun ray peeking through one of the trees, soaking up the warmth. All I thought about was that this was my happy place—a place I solely called mine. No one dared come near the falls—not when the Ashix swooped and dipped around in the sky, dropping down at any given time.

Closing my eyes, I took in the sounds and smells that surrounded me like I did each time I came here. Pine tar was strongest; overpowering any blooming flowers; it had to be dripping from a tree nearby. The sounds—birds chirping softly, crickets stringing their legs together to create musical harmony and serenity.

Crack. A branch snapped, and then another one shortly after, disturbing that peace.

I stood abruptly and discovered all the noise had

dropped; it was dead silent. Not even the crawl of an insect over dried leaves could be audible.

"He-Hello?"

No answer. The seconds ticked by in an agonizing slowness before yelling out again, "Hey--if someone is out there spying on a lady, that's not very nice, and I'm inclined to kick your ass. So I suggest you bugger off before I roast you."

There was still no response, but the even slower crawl of bumps scattered along my arms and prickling needles threaded themselves in the back of my neck as if someone was still lurking. They were hidden as I scanned my eyes among the foliage, not even the animals stirred.

Whoever it was must have been, was hiding up top of the falls. I was sure that's where the snapping of the sticks came from, but I wasn't stupid enough to go check it out. Rechecking my shoes while scanning my surroundings before returning to the forest and heading home, I found nothing and ran.

Finally, the rooftop of my home appeared, so I ran faster. I was relieved to spot Mom in her garden, plucking weeds aggressively. I chuckled to myself, and instead of disturbing her, I veered to the side of the house where my punching bags were set up.

The boulder was visible from where I stood, and instinctively I peered around for Beauty. She still wasn't in her spot. *Where the heck are you, girl? It's been a few days, and you have me worried.*

Walking over to the boulder, I checked the surrounding area for any fresh signs of her. Aside from the tall red grass surrounding the rock, she left no recent signs at all. It seemed more trampled than usual where I sat, and some grass even looked like it had been pulled up from the ground, which was unusual.

It had been the spot where I would sit in front of the large boulder and gaze out across the fields and trees as the sunset, before going inside most evenings, so part of it was caused by me, but the rest left me baffled.

Shaking my head, I walked back to my boxing bag and started wrapping my hands from the knuckles down to the wrist to keep them safe and add extra support. Once done, I stepped up to the bag and threw a one-two combo repeatedly until my knuckles ached.

On the last hit, a high-pitched scream reverberated from the front of the house near where my mother was tending to the garden.

Running towards the sound, I stopped abruptly and flapped my arms to keep myself upright. I almost fell forward when I took in the sight before me.

My mother was on the deck near our front door with the arm of a male around her neck. I immediately recognized the male in question from the village. He was the one with the eye patch that I bumped into outside of The Healing Shadows.

Trying to take in more of the surroundings, I didn't detect anyone else until another male shadow-jumped in next to the asshole I dubbed 'Patches.'

Goddess above, grant me strength.

I realized they both were Shadow Assassins. But the question remained: what the hell were they doing here, and why did they have my mother hostage? We were nobody of importance and had nothing these males could want.

"I don't know what you want, but you need to let my mother go now. We have nothing of value, he-" I said, but was rudely interrupted.

"Oh, but Raine, you do have something valuable here."

The male, Patches said. Being interrupted grated on my nerves, which led me not to hold my tongue.

"Yeah, I don't think so, asshole," I responded, but something else clicked in my head at that very moment. "Wait, how do you know my name?"

While the other male remained quiet, Patches smirked as he continued, "Well, I can't give away my secrets now, can I? Not before we get what we are being paid to retrieve for someone."

Looking at my mother, her face paled, and her eyes widened, glued to mine. Whatever was going on, it couldn't be good. Deep down inside, I understood they were here for me and not anyone or anything else. If they wanted my mom, they would have just snatched her and shadow-jumped out of there without a trace.

Peering at my mother, my brain ran a million miles an hour like the thoughts inside my mind were swirling in a tornado's wind. I needed to bluff our way out of whatever the heck would happen next and fast. She had to overcome their grip and run away from them; that's all I thought about. When Shadow Assassins were on the job, they didn't usually leave any eyewitnesses—not if this was some kind of kidnapping job, at least.

Gripping my hands into fists, I uttered vehemently to the males standing before me, "You will unhand my mother. I will not repeat myself. Take what you want from the house or garden, but leave us be."

"Tsk, Tsk, I do not think so, Raine. You see, if I let your mother go, then what leverage will I have to make you comply? You do understand what is going on, don't you, female? It was written across your face when you realized we were here for you." His grin widened even more, showing off those fangs again; his were longer than any other AshFieran's I had seen, and something stirred inside that I was not going to dissect at that moment.

First, Raine, save Mom; then you can figure out what's going on with your reactions to the male. Maybe we should ignore them completely; now wasn't the time to be an idiot.

"Okay, okay. Look," I started, with my hands raised in the air. "If I come with you, my mother goes free. I need assurance she is going to be safe."

"I can agree to this, but you must come here first," he said, gesturing for me to move forward.

I laughed at the way he must have thought I was naive enough to trust him, "No way, Patches, I'm not stupid. You let her go first, and then I will come."

"My name is Zynas, not Patches." He grunted. "Here's what I will do: I will take my arm out from around her neck, but she is not to move away until you are much closer."

My gaze had shifted to the other male, who kept an eye out and was now shifting side to side on his feet. His fingers were fidgeting together, and his focused intent was on the treeline. Was someone else here? Would someone be coming to save us?

I held onto that hope for a bit longer.

Eyeing the trees briefly, my attention came back to the front of my house. When I looked at my mother, a silent tear rolled down her cheek.

She spoke softly, "Raine, I love you with my very soul. The Goddess gifted me such an amazing daughter. No matter what happens next, you must run where you behold your safety."

She meant the waterfalls, the one place I believed to be safest and had a sense of kinship with, but everything had happened so rapidly that it took time for my slow brain to catch up.

Another male exited our house, glared his hateful eyes at me, strode up to my mother, and punched her in the stomach. She doubled over. I hadn't known a third male was lurking around. Did he shadow-jump into my home?

Looking back at my mother, a red stain became visible on her shirt where he had hit her, spreading as her breathing slowed and her eyes began fluttering. The male who punched her stood next to my mother with a dagger in his fist, dripping red onto the wood planks of our porch.

"NO! Mom NOO! Why, why, WHY?" I screamed, causing burning pain in the back of my throat, with a raspy cough following. Her faint smile was directed toward me, not quite seeing me, as she slumped in Zynas's arms.

Time slowed when I watched her eyes close for the final time. Remembering my mother's instructions, I didn't hesitate; I turned and ran. Voices ricocheted off the trees as the asshole, Patches, who still held onto my mother, yelled at the other male, "You fucking idiot, now we have to chase the female. He's going to be pissed you hurt Pandora. You realize that..."

It was all I could make out as I ran further and further away from my now-dead mother and the home I grew up in. I didn't do a leisurely run like I had that morning. No–all the strength I could muster from deep within was put into my speed. The blur from my eyes blocked my view of the trail ahead, along with the wind-whipped hair that came partially undone from my bun, flying around in my face.

I ran so fast that the loud rushing of the waterfall was getting closer already.

Almost there, you can do it, Raine. Just a little further, you can hide and figure out what to do next later.

I was clearly losing my mind since I had just been talking to myself and not paying attention. Branches snapped rapidly behind me, getting louder and closer. Whoever was following me was fast; I was sure that I had a good head start on them when I ran from the house: *thump, thump, thump, thump.* The steps were in time to my rapidly pounding heart, as the falls came into view.

A whooshing sound flew past my right side. A second later, the burning pain radiated in my upper right arm. *That motherfucker shot at me with an arrow! What the hell?*

As I turned my head and looked behind me, I realized the male was almost close enough to grab hold of my tank. Panic rose with bile in my throat. At this moment, all I could think about was, this was it. I was going to die like my mother.

Before turning around, another arrow flew past my face, missing it by inches and straight into my assailant's throat, dropping him into a heap instantly. The gurgling left the male's mouth, and all that ran through my mind was that I needed to turn my body back around.

It was already too late, though. I was too close to the ledge of the waterfalls and tumbled over to the sharp rocks and water below.

Accepting my fate was a fickle battle that I didn't want to give in to, as I fell, my body facing upward toward the sky, where I didn't allow myself to close my eyes. And on the ledge, there appeared a dark outline of a male looking over at me while I fell to my demise. In his hands, he held a bow, but the string was empty of any arrows. *Strange.*

Falling, I screamed inside myself, angry that I had lost the only remaining parent I had left in this world. Then, I was screaming on the outside, a natural reaction to the position of helplessness and the momentum of falling.

Time seemed to slow; my body hung suspended, and I should have already hit the water. Instead, I was being engulfed in shimmering darkness, and the suction of a tornado's vortex dictated which way my body would go. Panic settled around my heart, squeezing. I looked to the sky. The figure was still standing at the ledge, watching my body disappear; he was even further away. Then, nothing was visible in front of my face except the glittering black void. It overtook my entire body.

That darkness started reversing slowly, and instead of the whipping suction moments ago, the direction changed. Like the wind of a hurricane pushing me forward until a wooden floor came into view. I wasn't fast enough to brace myself as I slammed onto the floor on my side.

Groaning in pain, the burning in my arm radiated up, while my hip and shoulder throbbed. Lying on the floor, I shook from the rush of adrenaline zipping through my body, then I started coughing and gagging.

Closing my eyes, I focused on breathing in and out deeply to calm my body down. Slowly, it worked. The more I breathed, the more the shaking subsided. I no longer coughed or gagged on saliva. My breathing finally evened out after several minutes.

I took in my surroundings. I had landed in someone's home, and I needed to figure out what to say if they came in and witnessed a stranger in the middle of their living room. A fireplace sat in the middle of the furthest wall, and above, a mantle with several picture frames filled with people.

Getting up off the floor took some effort, but I managed. Walking closer to the mantle, I began to eye the pictures. Many of them showed two young girls throughout the years as they grew older. They looked familiar, and I figured out why when I reached the first adult one with three females, and in the middle of them all, the one person I loved my entire life.

Gasping, I took in the picture of my mother, her twin sister, and my grandmother. *Holy shit, they are all copies of each other.* Even my grandmother looked identical to mom and her sister, but older. My eyes started to water again, thinking of my mother. She would be so happy I had made it back here, but I believed this homecoming wouldn't go well when they found out she didn't make it with me. I hoped it went well, though; I needed some good in my life right now.

Later, I would need to figure out how exactly I got here, but right now, I needed to focus.

A clear shift in the atmosphere indicated they were approaching their home. Their energies matched perfectly with my mother's. It was more overwhelming with the two of them together. The scent of lavender and honey hit my nose first before two gasps sounded from behind.

I turned to the two women, who may or may not have realized who I was. I, however, doubted it as I looked like all three of them—a perfect copy of my mother and, by extension, my aunt and grandmother.

Chapter Three
Kalpheus

Taking a sip of the drink the bartender handed me, I let the smooth liquid flow down my throat. "Mmm," I hummed, nothing beats having a cold beverage after the day I've had.

Having to take the life of another wasn't something I cared for. The only way I was doing that sort of job was if the target was a terrible person out to hurt those less fortunate. In this case, the subject was an older male who kept killing his wives and then taking newer, younger ones shortly after their deaths.

The newest wife's brothers had contacted me, asking for help; they understood what he did to his wives and didn't want it to happen to this female, their sister. Her father had arranged the marriage in exchange for a lucrative business deal, and let's just say someone else in the family took care of him before I could. I had planned to offer to remove him for free; it would have been my pleasure if they had asked.

There was one rule we followed: you don't ever sell out your family. Loyalty was everything to a Shadow Assassin. We needed people to trust, even with our darkest secrets and fears that we wouldn't allow anyone else to see but those closest.

The family had told me they couldn't touch the older male who wanted to wed the daughter; it needed to look like an accident while leaving her unharmed and out of accusing fingers, so that's what I did.

While she was busy mingling with the party-goers of her wedding night, dancing individually with all six of her brothers to long, slow songs in front of witnesses, a calculated move, I ensured the rest happened while her new husband, ingested several drugs unbeknown to him, taking a tumble and landing face down in the water, all with help, of course, from yours truly.

Shortly after I ensured his demise, I made certain a concerned citizen reported seeing a body to one of the staff, and well, the rest was history.

I kept enjoying my drink when I regarded the shift, and suddenly, another male shadow-jumped to the seat next to mine.

"Kal, so good to see you, buddy." A hand clamped on my shoulder, squeezing lightly.

"Gezr, what is it you want?" He was never so pleasant with his greetings. He was here for a reason, and I wasn't in the mood for a drawn-out conversation. Straight to the point, that's how I liked things.

"Oh, come now, Kal. You know you're my favorite shadow-jumper, right?"

"Spit it out, Gezr, or I won't be your favorite for much longer," I grunted.

"I have a favor I need from you."

Lifting my eyebrows, I gestured for him to continue. It wasn't often he asked for favors.

"One of our comrades needs help, actually," he held up

his hands before I could shadow-jump out of the bar. I didn't like doing jobs for people I didn't personally have ties to.

He continued, "Just wait, please. Trouble is brewing outside one of the villages surrounding the city. Have you ever been to Martslocke?"

I shook my head, "No, I have never been to the little village, but I have knowledge of it."

"Alright, I can work with that. So, on the other side of the village, on the outskirts, lives a human witch with her daughter, who is half human and half AshFieran. Well, this female's husband, who is the young female's father, went missing several years ago on a perilous job. He was a vital and dangerous Shadow Assassin."

"Shit. Wait, what did you say his name was?" The answer was on the tip of my tongue; Stories of a shadow-jumper trickled into the close-knit groups surrounding the community of assassins. It was of a male who had left a human family behind in our world after going off on a job that he never returned from. It was rare for one of us to disappear without a trace, but not unheard of.

"I didn't, but his name was Lazarus, and he took on his wife's last name, Celestine." Gezr let out a deep sigh. "Look, the trouble coming their way is involved around whatever his business was, and my friend just wants some added protection. More for the younger female than anything."

I contemplated for a moment, but it didn't take long for me to reply. After all, it was apparent from the beginning that I would help two innocent females. "Alright, I'm in. Tell me where I need to go and what to expect."

"Well, that's the thing. I don't know what you will walk into and when the trouble might happen. All I have been told is Ca-," He started and then corrected himself swiftly.

"My understanding is that my friend said you must be the one to wait around the falls in case someone comes running that way. Several of us will be at different places in the forest surrounding their home, but he wanted you in particular at the falls."

Interesting. "When shall I go then?"

"Now."

I laughed, standing from my seat at the bar. Turning to look back at Gezr, but he was already gone. Clicking my tongue, *Gee–thanks, asshole, you didn't even tell me which falls I needed to be at.*

My first stop was jumping to the largest waterfall. Before moving on to the next one, I needed to access the area and assess if anything was amiss. It was an unusual gift I possessed. When I had a job lined up, my instincts led me in the right direction, allowing me to gauge a location's quality by the vibrations in the air. Nobody could ever tell me how it worked, just that it did, or maybe it was a connection to the Gods who once roamed AshFiera eons ago.

As soon as I cleared the electric darkness of my shadow-jump, the air let out a low humming, telling me I was in the right area. It was stronger than anything I had ever found before. But before making a move, I closed my eyes and let my body take in the sounds and smells.

I couldn't sense anything off by sound. It was all the expected natural melodies, birds singing for their mate, calling from the tree tops. A deer's chuff as they grazed the short grass that grew among the Sequoias. And the smaller animals skittering along the leaves that had fallen several months ago.

Taking a deep breath, I smelt the tar from the pines, clay from the ground, and a tinge of moss that most likely grew on the rocks surrounding the falls. Then, another, sweeter, alluring smell drifted toward me in the wind. *What in the Goddess's name is that amazing aroma, and where is it coming from?* It was the most intoxicating and addicting smell, sweet and rich, made of petals from jasmine and hints of honey.

Sweet Goddess, I needed to find out where that smell originated. My cock hardened in my trousers, my eyebrows pulled down in a frown toward the unruly appendage. I hadn't had that kind of reaction in a long time. And not from a single smell.

Creeping around the giant trees, I realized I had shadow-jumped to the very top of the waterfall. It was good, though; I took in further distances and would have more of an advantage if someone crept along.

What I didn't expect, as I rounded the tree closest to the edge of the falls, was a female. *Was this the young female I was meant to look after?* She was breathtaking, lounging with hands splayed behind her on a large boulder near the lower ledge of the falls. Eyes closed, and face tilted towards the sun rays.

Those rays illuminated her hourglass figure, causing her to look as if she were the Goddess herself. Long, dark chocolate hair with hints of golden honey highlights glowed from where I stood. I couldn't catch her eye color yet, but I was dying to find out if they lit up like the rest of her. Her beautiful, tanned skin indicated that she spent a lot of time outdoors, which was also reflected in the outfit she was currently wearing. A pair of black shorts that hugged thick thighs, I imagined those being wrapped around my waist. And a white tank that, if water splashed onto the right areas, her nipples would be visible.

Taking a step closer, my foot snapped a branch. *Shit, you idiot.* I was not paying attention and was too busy gawking at the female. Stepping behind the tree before she spotted me, I snapped another branch. *FUCK. What is wrong with me?* I was stealthy, not this clumsy doof that didn't even pay attention to where he was stepping.

A moment later, her feminine voice carried over to me; it was so right. My cock, already hard, was on the verge of bursting inside the dark trousers I wore. I needed to control myself quickly. I was acting like a teenage youngling again, about to touch a female for the first time.

"He-Hello?" She said, sounding unsure of herself at first. Even though my body was fighting itself, I stayed still. The urge to reveal myself and speak with her was growing, but I resisted.

"Hey, if someone is out there spying on a lady, that's not very nice, and I'm inclined to kick your ass. So I suggest you bugger off before I roast you." This time, her voice grew stronger and more sure of herself as she threatened violence —my kind of female. I would love to tangle with her. Show her a few moves that would allow me to pin her to the ground and fuck her senseless.

Shaking my head. I needed to snap out of it and focus. She must be the one I was tasked to protect. Something about her drew me in like a moth to a flickering flame. *I need to sort that out later*.

The crunch of foliage under someone's foot made me snap my gaze up as I watched her run opposite the falls and out of the forest. Her home must have been in that direction. Now that she was no longer around, I needed to scope the surrounding area. I waited a few minutes for my cock to soften before shadow-jumping to the edge of the forest in the same direction she disappeared to.

Standing at the edge, past the tall red grass in the short distance was a large yet cozy cottage home; it looked well-loved. I spotted the young female, my eyes drawn to her instantly. She was on the side of the house, looking toward a boulder on the forest's edge to my left. I hurled my eyes away from her as I took in more of the home. Another older female was in a garden, pulling weeds, and when she looked up in my direction, I froze. She was identical to the younger female; this must have been her mother. She was still looking over here and looking right at me, but she didn't seem startled that I stood on guard. Instead, she nodded, smiled, and returned to pulling the weeds.

I didn't stick around much longer, satisfied I had located the home of the females in question. I headed back to the falls and set up a good hiding spot high in one of the Sequoias, making sure to face the direction of the female's home.

Stretching my legs out on a large branch, I closed my eyes briefly, folding my arms over each other. I willed my body to sleep lightly just in case I was needed, but that sleep was short-lived when someone's high-pitched scream in the distance caught my attention. It was in the direction of the house.

Not long after, snapping and heavy breathing came from far off. I had excellent hearing; almost all of the Shadow Assassins did. So I readied my bow and arrow, which I took with me to every job where I needed to be hidden high up.

Then she appeared, the younger female, running with unshed tears in her eyes and wet, dirty streaks running down her cheeks and neck. Close behind her, an unknown male hastily chased her. I didn't know who he was, but a red mist glazed over my vision when he knocked an arrow, shot, and grazed her arm, causing blood to start dripping out of the flesh wound. Anger bubbled, and I didn't waste any time; I knocked my arrow and let it soar through the air and into the side of his throat. Not a clean kill and most certainly not a fast death as he gurgled over the blood that was pooling in his throat, blocking most of the air he was desperately trying to take in.

Taking my eyes off the dying male, I found the female was far too close to the end of the ledge. I tried shadow-jumping to grab her before she fell over. But it was too late. As I jumped to the ledge, she had already been falling toward the water below.

I glanced over and blinked in surprise. Behind the female was a shimmering dark portal slowly covering her like water. Her eyes were wide with fear, staring directly at me. I was finally able to see the color of her eyes. Even with fear in them, I was right. They were lit so brightly, the emerald green orbs sparkled with life until she was completely enclosed in the dark, and then she was gone.

Stepping away from the ledge, walking to the male who was lying on his back. Surprisingly, he was still clinging to his life. Pulling out my dagger, I crouched over his bloodied body, put the dagger to his throat under the protruding arrow, and growled, "You don't deserve peace in the next life. You touched what didn't belong to you, piercing her flesh. I hope what awaits you is an eternity of misery."

His eyes shifted to mine. He mustered a few slurred words: "Please. End. It."

I chuckled, "No, you don't deserve the courtesy. Now, you will bleed out slowly. Shouldn't be much longer anyway."

Sliding the dagger back into my sheath, I rose and headed toward the home to check the situation the older female was in. I didn't spot her mother at first, and I had a sinking feeling based on the dried, dirty streaks lining down the younger female's cheeks, which suggested what had happened. Caution was needed, though. The male couldn't have been the only one around, but there was only one way to find out.

Making it to the forest's edge, I crouched, staying in the shadows, taking in the view in front of me. A large red stain was left on the deck in front of the house, but nobody was in sight. At least no one was outside, and inside, several feet shuffled.

A lone male exited the home, cradling the older female in his arms. She was lifeless and had a sheet over most of her body except her head. He didn't waste time, briefly looking at her with pain etched along his face, he shadow-jumped with her lifeless body from the deck. All was silent, no other signs of others around, and the roaming footsteps inside the home ceased.

I needed to head back to the falls and track where the portal the younger female conjured had brought her. Its energy would call to mine, and I would mimic part of it. I didn't have it down to a science, and it wasn't always the most reliable. I hoped it would take me as close to her as possible, allowing my instincts to guide me in the right direction when I arrived.

As I reached the ledge again, Gezr shadow-jumped near me and collapsed to the forest floor.

"What the fuck happened to you, Gezr? You look rough." I said, rushing over to him and looking at his bloodied and already bruised face.

"It was an ambush, Kalpheus. They knew we were spread out, keeping guard on the home and the two females. A few of the males didn't make it, but most of us acted swiftly. Once we understood what was happening, we shadow-jumped to a central area to fend off the attackers."

He looked over at the now-dead male. "I see they also sent one your way."

I shook my head, "No, this one was chasing the female, and I got to him before he even knew I was here."

"Goddess, where is she?" He was looking around as if I had hidden her from sight.

"She's not here. She fell over the ledge and was engulfed in a dark portal. I think she created it without realizing it was her doing. She looked terrified. I was just about to try to track the energy to keep an eye on her, wherever she took herself."

Gezr blew out a deep breath. "Good, okay. At least she's not here, and no one will think of looking for her elsewhere for the time being. Keep me updated once you find her, and we will come up with a plan. She's more important than we realized, Kal. When you find her, protect her at all costs."

Nodding, I understood all too well she was essential, somehow—not only to whoever was trying to find her but now to me. I couldn't shake this feeling, an unforgettable and sparking connection. She might not have seen more or known the connection I tuned into, but I had to find her.

So I leapt right over the ledge. Diving into the depths, immediately the connection of the female's dark tendrils lingered from the portal, latching onto my energy and sinking in. Suddenly, I shadow-jumped outside an unfamiliar home in another realm. It was nestled nicely in a clearing surrounded by pine and oaks. The area seemed familiar, but I couldn't place it. So I hid myself in the shadows just inside the tree line, observing and thinking about what my next move would be.

Chapter Four
Raine

My aunt and grandmother stood in the doorway. I gave them a watery smile and a small, awkward wave.

"Pandora?" My aunt choked and immediately covered her mouth to stifle a sob.

Taking a deep breath, I introduce myself, "Actually, no. I'm Raine, Pandora's daughter. I'm sorry to barge in like this, but I seem to have just ended up in the middle of your living room."

I gave them both a tentative smile, shifting side to side on my feet, shoulders slowly bunching up, and waiting for them to stop gawking at me and say more than just my dead mother's name. Thinking about her made me sniffle while I played with my fingers.

Noticing my fidgeting fingers, my grandmother took a wary step toward me, testing my reaction to her moving closer like a person would do with a hurt animal. "Raine, such a beautiful name she gave you." Her smile was kind, and I let my shoulders relax.

"I think so, too. Mom said she named me Raine because

while she was in labor with me, all it did was pour water from the clouds above. And when I was born, it had finally stopped. She said it was the longest forty-eight hours of her and my father's life, waiting for my stubborn arrival." A tear slipped down my cheek as I gave a small smile, thinking about the time she used my birth as a bedtime story. It was raining outside, and the thunder had scared me so much that I wanted to sleep in bed with her. My heart ached at the memories. I would never make any more with her, and that realization left me breathless. Hearing the older woman's voice brought me out of my thoughts of misery, clouding my heart.

"Well, now that we know your name, we should probably introduce ourselves. I am your Grandma Gwenmyra. You can call me Gigi if you like, and that is your mom's twin sister, Samara," she said, pointing over at the female. No, not female, that wasn't right. She was a woman here. Something instinctively told me they referred to genders differently. The memory was trying to trickle its way out of the back of my mind, but I lost it. Looking over, Samara was still in the doorway, her mouth gaping open, staring at me.

"Yeah, Mom told me all about you and Aunt Samara in hopes that maybe one day we would come back to the human realm, Earth, and visit or maybe even stay." The slight smile I had a moment ago faded as I remembered who was missing. She would never step foot into this world or embrace her family. Or me again.

Then, I was being crushed by my grandmother, Gigi, who had her arms wrapped around me. I couldn't help it; the sob left me as I buried my face into her chest, another pair of arms encompassing both Gigi and me from behind. Looking over my shoulder, my eyes landed on Aunt Samara's beautifully familiar face. Our faces were close together.

She leaned in, placed her forehead against mine, closed her eyes, and sighed. I followed by closing my own in reflection.

Right here is where I was meant to be, my heart slowly being mended in the presence of these two women who had been missing my entire life.

The start of a cracked, missing piece of my heart stopped forming. It was fusing back together the longer they held me. Their hold on me was like sunshine pouring down from the heavens after a heavy rainfall. My body lightened, relieved.

We stood in front of the fireplace for a moment longer until my stomach growled loudly, and Aunt Samara laughed.

"It seems we need to solve something else that our magic can't soothe. Come, my darling niece, let us head to the kitchen and grab you a bite to eat." Grabbing my hand, Aunt Samara pulled me to the kitchen without waiting for a response.

"You sit here on the stool, and I will whip something up quickly."

Samara began cooking scrambled eggs, toast, and bacon when Gigi walked through the doorway and sat on the stool beside mine at the kitchen island.

"Raine, we are so happy to have finally met you." She started, but I knew there was more she wished to say, and she was trying to be sensitive, given the state I was currently in. "But we need to know what happened to you and your mom. She's not with you, and it's been so long since she was whisked away from us."

Tears began to well in my eyes as I looked at Gigi, "She didn't make it. Some males–men held her hostage. I still don't understand why, but they were at our home for me, not Mom. It was like she knew exactly what was going to happen next. She made me promise to run and not look back, no matter what. And then th-they." I couldn't finish; it was too hard to speak while I imagined that knife being buried into her stomach, the crimson red dripping from the assassin's blade when he pulled it out.

"Shh, it's all right now. You are here and safe with us." My grandmother soothed, gently brushing her hand through my hair. Her touch was an instant relief as the building despair vanished. Like smoke blowing in the wind away from me, clearing the ache in my heart and replacing it with warmth.

I couldn't help but ask, "What is that? When you touch me, both of you. Why do I feel the sadness dissipate and almost become non-existent?"

Gigi answered first, "It's our gift. Samara and I are healers, both physically and emotionally. I apologize if we have overstepped, but when we sensed your distress, our gifts acted on their own, especially since you are our kin."

"I see; Mom's gift was different from the two of you," I said. "She could grow a wicked garden. Her plants grew faster and larger. Not only that, but they stayed fresh for much longer. Leaving a harvest to last months longer than it should, and even longer if you properly preserved the produce."

"She was magnificent and very much connected to the Goddess here. It wasn't only plants she had kin with. It was the animals as well." Gigi said, nodding.

"I-I didn't know that; she had never connected with the animals back home. At least not that I knew of." I thought back to growing up, and I never remembered seeing her interact with other animals besides Beauty. But that was only after Beauty had started protecting me and watching over the property.

Samara finished cooking the breakfast meal even though it was evening and would constitute dinnertime. I looked at her with a question on the tip of my tongue, and she shrugged with a wistful expression on her face.

"Sometimes we like to eat breakfast for dinner and dinner for breakfast. Makes things more interesting instead of the same boring meals." She winked at me.

I smiled; she must have been the rebel twin. Mom was so organized and dead set in her ways that she rarely strayed from her routine or what she knew worked.

We quickly ate—well, I did. I hadn't eaten since earlier and didn't have lunch because of what had happened. The energy was rapidly dissolving, and I stifled a yawn into the back of my hand, trying to keep it hidden from the two women.

Gigi didn't miss it, though. "Come now, child, let us get you into your new room. I hope you don't mind, but the only spare room we have is your mom's old room. It still has everything she had ever collected since childhood. We didn't want to touch it if she ever returned to us and needed a place to rest."

"Thank you, Gigi. I would love to go to bed; I'm exhausted." I gave her a small smile and followed her to my mother's room. She didn't linger long. Instead of saying goodnight, she kissed my forehead and closed the door softly.

There, I was left alone with my thoughts, and they started to turn dark without the positive energy that both women emitted. I began to dislike the feeling of having any happiness. It felt too much like I was betraying my mother's memory so soon.

I didn't want to feel anything but grief, sorrow, anger, and pain. All those emotions I tried to embrace, and ever so slowly, I let that happiness leech out and replaced it with a steel wall. I surrounded my heart with a thick liquid barrier.

I didn't realize the happiness seeped out in a rush until I was sitting on the ground, gasping for air.

While I sat, catching my breath, I turned to the mirror that was propped up in the corner of the room. My back was at the end of the bed, and I looked at my reflection. My usually bright emerald green eyes, which I shared with my mother, had darkened to a deep mossy green. I wasn't startled by the change; instead, I embraced their darkness and briefly felt that control was mine, that I looked less like my mother.

And maybe if I didn't resemble her completely, I could get over the suffocation of losing her.

But then guilt, the fickle emotion it was, entered unwillingly at how I could just leave her to die alone with those heartless monsters.

I had been training with my father for most of my life until he disappeared, and then I continued that training with Uncle Cass.

Uncle Cass—he probably has no idea what happened.

And when he did decide to drop by, he would see that no one was at our little cottage, and he would likely notice the pool of blood that was left behind. I wondered if he would come looking for us, for me. It was possible, but I knew he wouldn't find us. Not unless he saw and asked one of the Seers who resided in the city of Ozryn. I learned about the mysterious Seers in the cities. Mother would talk about them once in a while, so I understood what magical entities those people possessed.

I didn't want to be found by Cassius, though. I wasn't going back, and I didn't even have a safe home to return to.

Looking at him would remind me too much of everything I had lost.

Crumpling in on myself, fisting bits of my hair, the anger bubbling to the surface, I felt my body getting hot again like it had when I was younger, when I hadn't yet learned how to control my temper by other means. And it seemed I had forgotten everything Uncle Cass taught me to control those wild, untamed emotions.

My breath picked up speed, in and out, faster and faster until I screamed. I let my fist connect with the mirror sitting in front of me. The shattering crashed loudly, and shortly after, I could detect running footsteps down the hall and the bedroom door being flung open.

I sat on the floor of my mother's old room, arms wrapped around my legs, tucking them close to my body, and stared at the ground where the glass lay.

Gentle hands were on my face, wiping away the tears from my cheeks. My head was tilted to look at my aunt's face. The identical face I looked at growing up. Only this wasn't my mother, and the pain slicing through my heart was a jagged-edged knife digging further in. Concern was etched on her face, and she didn't say anything for the moment. She held my cheeks, and I felt her prying, trying to overcome the barriers I had erected earlier.

"Raine, you have to let me in. I can make you feel better and lessen the pain in your heart. Please, let me in." She begged, her powers were still trying to penetrate my mind and heart. But I didn't want that; I wanted her to leave instead. Let me drown in sorrow.

"No, I don't want to feel anything but this. Just let me feel this." I quietly sobbed.

She looked deep into my eyes and nodded. Getting down on her knees, she held me close. I let her, but didn't embrace back; it all felt too raw. She let me sit there for what seemed like hours as the time crawled by.

A while later, with the glass cleaned up and the remainder of the mirror removed from the room, I was lying in bed staring at the wall. I couldn't fall asleep yet; it was late.

Back on AshFiera, if I couldn't sleep, I would sneak out of my room and look at the stars. Most nights, the sky would dance with the Aurora Borealis. I wondered if we were in an area where it would do that here.

Deciding I needed fresh air anyway, I got up and started to sneak down the hall. I found the door and the flooring in this house were silent. My shoulders sagged at the unfamiliarness.

If I wanted anything to be ordinary, it was that, but this wasn't my home, and I was so painfully reminded of that, so I kept walking down the hall and toward the back patio door.

Opening the sliding glass door to the backyard, I shivered slightly. It was cold this evening, and I needed something better to cover myself with. Looking over the living room, I went to the couch and grabbed a throw blanket lying across the back, wrapping myself up before heading out the door I had left open.

Walking out, I noticed a concrete patio while spying a lounge chair with a pillow half haphazardly lying on it. My body moved on its own, heading in that direction, lying myself down on my back as I faced the darkened sky.

I could view the stars clearly; this evening was perfect. Not a single cloud was found in the sky, and the moon, a sliver, emitted hardly any light. The sky held so many more stars here, but I felt disappointed that no beautiful pinks, purples, greens, or blues were dancing among them. My body was calmer now than earlier in my mother's old room, and while I looked up at all the twinkling stars, another shiver went through my body, and I let out a breath. The air fogged before my face from the heat and cold colliding.

At that moment, I wished it had been warmer so I could stay out here and admire the crowded sky that was dotted differently than back home, but I was getting too cold and needed to sleep anyway.

In the morning, I planned to apologize to Gigi and Samara for breaking Mom's mirror and for having to clean up the mess I made.

Sitting up from the lounge chair, I started heading back inside, but paused when the familiar prickling crawled up my neck and to the base of my head. I spun around and looked into the tree line. I didn't pick out any movement and didn't catch anything amiss, either. Shaking my head, I turned around and quickly went inside to crawl under the covers, needing to forget the disastrous day I had endured.

THE MORNING SUN shone through the curtains that I hadn't closed the night before. It was so bright, and the rays were blinding through my eyelids, that I threw the blanket over my head and groaned.

There was a light knock on my door a moment before a feminine voice spoke. "Raine, are you awake?" It was Samara. I should have gotten up and opened the door, but instead, I just uttered the words under my covers, "Yeah, I'm awake."

The light squeak of the bedroom door opening told me my aunt had let herself in once I alerted her to being roused.

"Hey, sleepy head," she said as the bed dipped from her sitting. "I wanted to check on you and see if you wanted to come with me somewhere."

I pulled the blanket down just enough to show my eyes so I could look at her and raised an eyebrow, silently telling her to keep speaking.

"I was thinking last night, after you broke the mirror, that I recognized that anger anywhere. Like you can't control this world and the things that happen, I had those same feelings after your mom disappeared, and I found an outlet for myself. A place I like to go when I want to be around others without being bothered. A place that allowed me to let some steam off," she said.

I pulled the blankets down all the way and sat up in bed, interested in where she was going with this.

"We have a club called 'The Moonbright,' and I have a close friend who works out, trains people, and the best part is he owns it, but it's a fighting club, and before you ask, yes, it's completely legal as long as you sign an injury waiver. They will let you train and even compete in fights." She said, patiently waiting for my response.

Would I want to be involved in something so similar to what I enjoyed back home?

It would feel nice to throw my fists into something or even someone. I had my answer already, but I didn't understand why I was hesitating to tell Aunt Samara. Maybe it was the lingering guilt of doing something so normal shortly after everything happened, which shook me from yet another depressing thought.

A trickle of excitement coursed through my body at the prospect of finally relieving the mounting pressure.

"Yes, I would love for you to take me. I used to do that sort of stuff with my father before he disappeared on a job years ago, and then I had Uncle Cass, who was Mom's best friend. He wasn't actually my uncle, but I liked calling him that growing up. He trained me once a week up until now." I looked at her, and she was smiling so vast it was a little scary. "What?" I asked.

Shaking her head, she responded, "Nothing, it's amazing that you have one of my traits. I wonder what else you have of mine and your mother's."

"Well, since learning from you guys that Mom was connected to nature, I feel I have a special connection with animals as well. Back home, I have an Ashix named Beauty. Mom said she's a smaller version of your mythical dragons. She's a beautiful pearlescent white with burnt orange eyes." I said with a smirk, thinking about my sassy girl. "She is fierce and doesn't allow anyone around her, and she used to let mom around her, but only if I was with her."

Samara smiled at me, "Then the Goddess has also blessed you. Have any other powers manifested yet?" Curiosity shone through her eyes. It didn't feel like I was being interrogated like Uncle Cass would sometimes do, so I answered the best I could.

"Mmm, yes and no. I thought I could feel something inside, but it had just vanished a few days before the incident. Once, I had sparked some purple lightning from my fingertips before my dad disappeared. Scared the shit out of me; I could feel the electricity zing through my hands. It was weird and slightly uncomfortable." I didn't mention the day I thought I witnessed purple lightning enter through my mom's eyes, and coincidentally, that was just the other day when we were at the village.

"Alright, well, there is some breakfast in the kitchen for you. And no, I promise it's not a dinner item. I put out a few things for you to choose between." She smiled, got up from the bed, and headed out the door.

I sat on the bed brushing my fingers through my long hair, getting snagged on a snarl as I waited for my body to wake up more. I couldn't be lazy any longer this morning, though. We had somewhere to be and someone to meet who would hopefully let me use his club without identification from this world.

I could feel the buzz of excitement running through my body as I considered the many prospects of how I would fit into this world. Hopefully, this club was one of them.

Stretching as I stood, I quickly got ready and went to the kitchen. And when I entered, I looked toward the island. On the counter were apples, bananas, bread, peanut butter, and what looked like homemade oat bars.

They looked so similar to the ones Mom used to make me.

Aunt Samara walked into the kitchen just as I reached for one of the bars.

"Oh, those are my famous oat bars. Your mom used to devour an entire sheet within a day or two." She laughed.

Looking at her, I took a bite and moaned, "Oh my goddess, Mom used to make these for me all the time. These are my favorites, and they taste the same." I swallowed not only the oats but the lump that formed in my throat. "She loved you very much, Aunt Samara. I didn't know you used to make these for her; she never told me where she got the recipe from."

She looked at me with tears in her eyes, smiling, "Well, I'm sure glad that she figured out how to make them and that I earned the honor to spoil you with the bars as well. Now, hurry up because I called ahead to Gage and informed him we were coming. He's very excited to meet you." She finished with a slight blush.

I didn't let it slide. I loved teasing my mom about the constant flow of men who all tried but failed to catch her attention when we visited the village.

"Aunt Samara, look at that blush you got going on. Oh, is Gage a male caller?"

"No–no, nothing like that. Gage is a very good friend of mine. We have never gone into anything more, and I don't think we ever will." She said, the red stain on her cheeks deepening. "Okay, finish up, missy, and I will meet you in the truck."

I giggled as she practically ran out of the kitchen toward the front of the house. I let myself have that little bit of joy. My emotions were all over the place, and it gave me whiplash. I needed to take it one day at a time, I decided. And when I was in my dark place, I needed to let myself go through it.

My head couldn't grasp the reality of ever getting over leaving my mother. It was too late. She was gone, and I would never see her again. I wouldn't even be given a chance to give her a proper burial. Leaving me unsure of how to get back to AshFiera in the first place, and secondly, I had several assassins after me in that world.

Chapter Five
Raine

Aunt Samara and I pulled up to a large building just outside Lunaris Falls's city limits, just a short distance from home.

On our way to the Moonbright Club, she told me about the city. It was full of witches and warlocks, along with the occasional human. Being one of the largest magic-led cities in the country, it held over one hundred thousand people and counting, as more and more of the magic folks were drawn to the ever-expanding cultures within.

I wasn't sure if I would feel comfortable venturing alone without Gigi or Samara by my side. Still, the club's location seemed easy enough to navigate, even if the building was large and intimidating.

I had never been to the city of Ozryn on AshFiera before and had only experienced the small village of Mart-slocke, where my home had been located. This place was a massive shock to the system.

After getting out of the truck and standing on the side-walk, I leaned down to talk with Aunt Samara, as she was still working on getting out and being around Gage. "Come on, Samara. Quit being a scaredy cat. The man of your dreams awaits us." She must have had a massive crush on him and was scared to act on her feelings, not wanting to tell him. My goal was to fix her singlehood status to taken. She didn't suspect I was up to anything yet, and I wouldn't tell her what I was planning.

We both walked through the door, my arm slung through hers, when I heard a man's deep voice yell from across the gym. "Sam! You're here! Just wait a few moments, and I will be right there." His boisterous voice carried over all the equipment to us.

"Sam, huh?" I gave her a knowing look.

"Yeah, he shortened my name a while ago," she grumbled.

"So, does that mean I can call you Sam, too?" Giving her a sweet smile, I fluttered my eyelashes at her.

She rolled her eyes in exasperation. "I suppose only if it will prevent you from pestering me any further about Gage."

"You got it, babes." I gave her a wink. It absolutely wouldn't stop me from wiggling any more information out of either one.

Gage finished whatever he was preoccupied with. When I spotted him jogging over to us from across the room, his face creased into a sizeable, cheesy grin, his sparkling eyes fixed on Sam.

Oh, this is going to be fantastic.

It was obvious, he had the hots for my aunt. I had to wonder why he hadn't made a move for her. I guess there was only one way to find out: when she left, I'd confront him.

"Hey, Gage. Thanks for meeting with us this morning.

This is my niece, Raine." Aunt Sam uttered, trying to hide the blush that slowly crept into her cheeks

"Raine, it's a pleasure to meet you. Although I didn't realize Sam had a niece at all." Gage said.

"Oh, yeah. I hadn't a clue I had a niece until yesterday when this lovely little bird dropped into our home." Looking at me, she smirked and folded her arms over each other.

Her stance made me giggle, so I replied, "Yes, quite literally dropped into your living room, Aunt Sam."

Gage laughed, giving my aunt a huge, toothy smile and his utmost attention drawn solely to her.

"Anyway, Gage, I need a favor. I understand you've stopped working with people to focus on your own projects, but Raine could really use someone to help release some of the built-up aggression. Like what I had dealt with when we first met." Sam said.

Gage looked at Samara with a lopsided grin and replied, "You could just ask to hang out again, Sam. You never come around anymore." His comment made my aunt blush fiercely, opening and closing her mouth like a fish caught out of water.

I was crossing my fingers; I had always worked better with someone than being alone while training. It's why Uncle Cass would come over once a week to ensure I was still on track and didn't slack off, correcting any postures or balances that seemed out of place, even showing me a few new moves every so often that I could incorporate with a deadly weapon. Of course, all those hours of training didn't help me when all I did was run away from the danger when it came down to it.

Gage looked at me with a new sense of purpose and gave me the best news I could have gotten since yesterday's ordeal. "Alright, kid, but I can only do it once a week. You can come in here anytime you want to use the machines. I'll make sure we get you set up with a VIP membership on the house."

I cleared my throat before speaking, emotions on the rise as I was granted access to the one thing I needed to keep my body strong and my mind free of the lingering guilt that would likely remain for an untold time. "Aunt Samara–Sam mentioned that if I signed a waiver, I might also be able to participate in competitive fighting? I would be interested in doing that, too, if possible."

"She did now, did she?" He looked over at Sam and then back at me, contemplating. "Well, let's see what you can do before heading in that direction, but we can keep it on the table. Not many women do competitive fighting, but I sense a few men who wouldn't be bothered to fight someone of the opposite sex."

I nodded, smiling like I won the grand prize in a gambling game back in Marteslock, which I wasn't allowed to be near, but would still sneak a peek when given the chance. Adrenaline started to spike in my veins, so I asked, "When can we start training? Does it work now? Because I'm free. Sam, you're free too, right?"

An exploding laugh bubbled out of my aunt, "Girl, you need to slow your roll. I'm sure Gage is busy today, but I can drop you off tomorrow before I head to do some errands if that works better."

"Today works great, Raine. I wouldn't mind seeing where your skills are at." Gage butted in.

I squealed a high-pitched noise. I couldn't believe my luck. My body was itching to release some of the built-up anger and grief from yesterday. "You don't mind, do you, Sam? If you wanted to, you could get those errands done today. Or sit here with us ogling over the buff men in here."

She glared at me briefly and addressed Gage, "Well, if you seriously don't mind. I could use this time to run around, as Raine mentioned, and leave you both to it."

"Really–Sam, I don't mind hanging out with your niece," said Gage.

"Okay, if I'm not back in time, will you call me when you are almost finished? Raine doesn't have a phone yet." Sam mentioned, adjusting her purse and digging around for the keys she had just had a few moments ago.

He nodded, giving Aunt Sam a dazzling smile, "Of course, but once I get into the zone with someone, we will likely get lost in it."

"Awesome. Well, Raine, don't get into too much trouble, and try not to hurt Gage." Before we could respond, she twirled around and headed out the door, jogging to the driver's side of her truck.

I turned my attention back to Gage. He gazed admirably at Sam while she sat in her old pick-up, probably fiddling with the radio or phone. I cleared my throat to grab his attention.

"So, before we start, I know we have to do warm-ups, but I need to throw this out there 'cause watching the two of you is hilarious, and Aunt Samara is too nervous to do anything herself when it comes to you."

"What do you mean? What is she too nervous to do?" Gage asked curiously.

"She's nervous around you; no idea why, though. But she has a crush on you one hundred percent. You should ask her out. It's quite obvious to me that you also fancy her, with the way your eyes take her in," I said, stretching my arms above my head.

"Oh–well, thanks, Raine. I will keep that in mind. Now, let's begin that warm-up you mentioned. I think running on the treadmill will be a good start to increase your heart rate."

We did just that. Both Gage and I ran for a long while. He had great stamina, and I needed to work on mine. By the end, I was breathing hard, sweat dripping down my face, while Gage was next to me with only slightly elevated breathing and minimal sweat. Afterward, he showed me some of his favorite weight stations he liked to use to help build muscle.

I must have been missing weight training back in AshFiera, because it was amazing; I could feel the burn in my arms and legs after completing just a few reps. Gage suggested that I focus on one part of my body per day, especially if I was planning on coming every day anyway. He didn't want me to burn out and get overly exhausted and sore before the real hand-to-hand training began.

And then, he took me into a separate room I hadn't seen when we first arrived. It was an ample open space with several elevated boxing rings dotted throughout. In the back of the gigantic building, a large archway led further back, where I laid eyes on a much larger elevated stage.

That must have been where the matches were held.

Gage noticed where I was looking and waved me to follow him. I guessed I was being led on a tour of the boxing area when he stopped just inside the archway.

"That's where we do all of our big matches." He said, pointing to the ring. I had been right, and elation rose as I imagined myself inside those ropes, pounding my fist into flesh.

My eyes scanned the room from the ring to the bleachers and chairs. Some open spaces were intended for those who wanted to stand. It was incredible. No wonder they had to have such a vast building and keep it outside the city. No way any place in or near the city had enough space for all this, and parking included.

"Gage," I began, "Thank you for taking me on and helping. I had a lot of things happen in such a short time that I'm not ready to talk about yet, but I needed this kindness." I said, quickly wiping a tear that had escaped when I thought of my mother and the agonizing realization that I would never see her and never return home.

"Kiddo, I am happy to help. I was available for your aunt when she was in a dark place and needed an outlet. She grew into quite the woman that I have admired from afar." His smile was slightly sad, but his eyes lit up. "But not for much longer, thanks to your openness. Look, I know Sam will be here soon, but if you want to take one of those boxing bags home, you can help yourself."

"Thanks, I think I will take you up on that. I might not be able to come here every day since I don't have a clue how to drive and don't want to burden Aunt Sam too much." I said.

Gage was right, too. Aunt Sam walked in shortly after we disassembled one of the bags to make it easier to transport in her truck. After loading the equipment, I waved to Gage, who was watching us out of the club's large window.

We sat in silence on the ride home. It was peaceful, and I kept my gaze out the window, watching the trees pass by in a blur.

It had been a short trip back home, as Gigi and Aunt Sam had lived not too far from the club but further from the city. If I were being honest, I didn't mind and had already been used to growing up outside of a village in AshFiera.

As I got out, I immediately unpacked the boxing bag and brought it to the back of the house. After reassembling it, I aimed a few shots at the body for a thorough test. I decided to get back into my routine tomorrow. Today felt so good, letting the stress melt away with the sweat that poured out of my body.

So, for the next few weeks, I built up my routine; I would wake up before the sun and go for a long run, come back, throw some punches at the bag, and visit Gage once a week. Sometimes, he would encourage me to go and train with him extra in a week, and I usually took him up on it.

I started building a new life and got to know Gigi and Aunt Sam better. They loved to travel and had been planning an overseas trip before I arrived.

Things had been going great until the first match I fought in. It was against a woman named Jen. She was one of the toughest females in the club, so I figured I would feel comfortable going up against her. In actuality, I was the toughest woman in the club—too vigorous, in fact, since I ended up putting her in the hospital after only a few hits.

She ended up with a concussion and broken ribs as a result.

The incident tore me apart with guilt, and I vowed never to fight another human woman again. And I hadn't competed in another match since the incident either. After that, I stopped going to the club to meet with Gage altogether. I spent most of my time in bed replaying the hits repeatedly for the next few weeks. It ate a hole through my every waking consciousness.

"Raine," my aunt spoke through the door, startling me while I had zoned out. "You can't keep yourself cooped up all day and night. You're going to make yourself sick."

"Go. Away." It was the only thing I mustered to say at the door; anything more was an effort.

"No flipping way, little lady," she said before she swung the door open so forcefully that it smashed into the wall, and the door handle left a tiny round indent in the drywall from the impact.

"Really? You just dented my wall, Aunt Samara." I sneered, hoping she would go away and leave me alone.

"I don't give a crap. Get. Up. You are going to eat some breakfast, and then your ass is going to go out for a run. I'm aware that it usually helps ease your mind, so I don't want to hear any excuses today. Afterward, you will punch on that bag of yours a few times and then come in and tell me how you feel when you're done." Aunt Sam chastised.

Slowly blinking at her, I rolled over and covered my head with the blanket.

At least it was covered until she grabbed it and yanked it off me.

"Hey! Give those back!" I snarled at her.

"No–Up–Now. I don't care how grumpy you get with me; you will thank me later. And if you don't get up, I will gather some ice water and pour it on you." Sam's face was a mask of fury, but I could tell she was trying to hold back her smile. She was enjoying antagonizing me with the possibility of being drenched in cold wetness.

"Okay, Okay. Jeez, I'm getting up, bossy pants. You sound like my mother."

Glaring at me the same way my mother had, she threw the blankets at my face, and I barely dodged them. Staring after her retreating form, my mouth gaped open, unable to speak. It was like I was having deja vu, causing me to wince internally.

Delaying the inevitable would only cause her to come

back here that much faster, and I didn't want to find out if she would throw ice water on me. So I got up, got dressed, and headed outside to do my first run in weeks.

By the time I made it back to the designated workout area that Gigi and Aunt Sam had decked out for me, I was exhausted. I looked around at my space and smiled, already feeling myself come back as the endorphins kicked in.

She sure knows me well, I thought. I remembered what she had said to me back in my room earlier. I would need to thank her and then listen to her gloat.

Wiping the sweat from my face with a towel, I eyed my bags. Gage had brought over a few more after I first started training with him, as I tended to be a little too hard on them, like I had been back home, and Mom would have to stitch them back together.

Thinking of her caused a lump to form in my throat. That happened often when I would think about her. I didn't know how long it would take for my heart to hurt less whenever I thought about her. Maybe it never would.

I walked over to the bags and started punching, closing my eyes and trying to focus on the one-two combo. Drifting into a rhythm, I was able to sink into my mind and think about the time mom showed me 'The Ashix Waterfalls' for the first time. It had been after Father disappeared. She wanted to show me something beautiful, a place she hoped I could go to at any time to escape the anger and hurt, and just be alone.

She told me how her people back on Earth would use the waterfall's natural flow to help revive or find their inner magic. The water had even helped a few witches and warlocks, who had been on the brink of death, giving them enough healing to make it to a hospital for further help. Mom also said that if someone hadn't yet manifested their powers, the falls would help find and bring forth those powers to aid them temporarily if they were ever in trouble.

They were such beautiful stories that I always felt the intensity and importance of the water and the falls.

Feeling several wet drops hit my hands, I finally realized I had stopped hitting the bags. I looked down at those hands, clenching and unclenching them several times. I had decided then and there that enough was enough, that I would stop feeling pity and self-loathing for myself. It was no way to live, so I laid in those bags with everything I had.

Each punch was more brutal until my last hit, which was so hard I sent the bag flying. Breathing heavily with everything I had, I screamed at the top of my lungs. Screaming so hard my voice began to crack, my knees landed on the ground hard.

Silence surrounded me, aside from my breathing. It felt good, though, to let all of that be free.

Feeling my body slowly relax, I huffed out a laugh.

Then, a snap of a branch echoed from the woods in front of me. My eyes darted up, and I stared into the shadows, waiting for any movement or noise. I felt it again, like at the falls on AshFiera, tingling up my neck. Someone was in the shadows, watching.

"I know you are out there," I shouted towards the darkness, shaking, my hands formed into fists at my side.

More silence greeted me. I kept staring into the woods, willing anything or anyone to show themselves. I didn't know what I would do if they came forward. At that moment, I silently vowed to myself that I would fight back and not run this time. I would face whatever came.

Another branch snapped, and a small rabbit ran out from a bush further inside the tree line. A breathy giggle left my mouth. It was silly to think I was yelling at a poor rabbit that was only trying to scrounge around for food.

Shaking my head, the crunch of gravel caught my attention as a truck turned into the driveway. I frowned, not remembering in all the weeks that I had been here if Gigi or Aunt Sam had had any visitors before. Usually, they were off in the city visiting one person or another, leaving the house silent for hours.

As the truck approached the house, I saw that it was Gage. I hadn't spoken to him in a while. I was sure Aunt Sam told him all about my reclusiveness these past few weeks.

He had finally worked up the courage to ask her out, and they had been seeing each other ever since. I was incredibly happy for them both and a little smug that I was the one to make it happen.

Gage parked the truck on the side of the house, got out, and headed to the back, where I was with my equipment.

He stopped and whistled, "What happened over there, Raine?" He was pointing in the direction where the bag had landed.

Shrugging, I answered honestly, "Hit it too hard. I guess I had too much pent-up energy and was saving it for my bag."

"Well, I am happy to see you out and about. Sam called me and said you went on a run, so I figured I would head out here to find you." His tone was gentle, reminding me that I had missed him over the last few weeks. He was like a big brother, always giving me life advice and trying to help me when the differences between our worlds confused me.

For instance, Earth had many more vehicles and technologies here than in AshFiera. Even the big city of Ozryn had limited transportation and little technology. It was something I was still trying to wrap my head around.

"So," he said, tucking his hands into his pockets. "I have some news I thought I would share that hopefully interests you."

"Gage–look, I'm sorry for ignoring you all these weeks, but if you came here to try to get me back in the ring, the answer is going to be no," I said, walking away to grab the bag that had been flung a few feet away.

I didn't make it far when Gage grabbed the bag to draw my attention to him. "Look, I understand you don't want to hurt anyone else, but what if I told you The Moonbright was hosting a two-day competition where you worked your way up from fight to fight? It would only be men except for you. Bragging rights are involved for the winner and free food from that burger joint you love so much."

"How in the hell does that work, Gage? And are you bribing me with food? Because it might be working," I asked incredulously, crossing my arms and raising an eyebrow.

"Maybe. But the guys suggested inviting you. It's an all-male competition, and you would be the only woman. They've seen how much you have grown and how well you handle yourself against me, and frankly, they want a chance to impress you."

His face told me he wasn't too thrilled about that. Some of the guys at the club had been respectful, but they often tried to distract me when I showed up to train with Gage. It was flattering and a nice change from Martslocke, where no males would even look my way.

"Can I think about it?" I asked, eyeing the bag, itching to hang it back up and go another round.

"Yeah, kiddo, of course. If you need a training buddy, I'm here; just let me know. And if you do decide to come, it will be in two weeks, starting on Friday and going all day Saturday."

"Thanks, Gage, for checking on me, even if it was because Aunt Samara told you I had emerged from my cave," I said, rolling my eyes.

Gage smiled while he hung the bag back up for me. Hugging me before heading back to his truck and leaving.

Knowing what I needed to do, I returned to hitting the bags. I sent a few punches, and the resounding thuds echoed across the trees as each one soared, bringing forth a new thought.

Thud, I was going to the competition, *thud-thud,* and I was going to kick a bunch of men's asses, send them flat on the floor, and maybe bruise a few egos while I was at it. *Thud.*

Giggling at that thought and working up a sweat while daydreaming about winning against the men and eating juicy, delicious burgers. I didn't have to think about it long after Gage left. I was going to the competition, and I was going to kick a bunch of men's asses.

Chapter Six
Kal

It was interesting to see the realm that the female had traveled to. Having been here several times in the past myself, and even taking up residence nearby, I knew this would make it easier to keep an eye on her. It was perfect, but what were the odds?

I recalled what Gezr said when he first asked me to oversee this young female's safety. He mentioned that his friend specifically requested me. Was this part of the reason for such a request? Did he perceive my travels to the human realm on occasion? I had so many questions, but there were no males present to answer them when needed. It was irritating to me not to have all the pieces to the puzzle.

If I were a different male, it would be detrimental to my life. However, I thrived on the complicated messes that would pop up unexpectedly. Maybe that was another reason the unknown male chose me to protect her. I was well known for getting out of dicey situations.

Sitting here in the tree line, I chuckled to myself. The females in this family liked to ensure they had plenty of trees in their backyard. It provided me with much-needed cover to be invisible during the day or night.

Sounds of movement came from inside the house. It was mostly quiet apart from the young female grunting in pain one moment, and the next, she was coughing and gagging.

My body was beginning to move toward the house when I had to stop myself. Crunching on gravel indicated a car was heading toward the house. I stood still, poised at the ready to shadow-jump to the front if need be—if she needed me.

After the vehicle stopped on the side of the house, two females emerged, walking around the house and up to the front door. The wind blowing towards my position let me catch their scent easily—lavender and honey, nearly the same as the young female. They must be the female's kin. Slowly, I backed into the woods, releasing a sigh. Relief coursed through my body. She would have someone to help her grieve for the time being until I could reveal myself.

I waited for a while outside, keeping guard. From the sounds of it, the three females got acquainted while inside. Once I felt it was safe enough, I decided to head over to the place I kept here on Earth.

Jumping was easy enough; I imagined my cabin's wrap-around porch and the wooden swing attached to its ceiling in my mind, materializing the vision in front of me.

It was instantaneous. I appeared in front of my home, away from home. Looking around, I ensured everything was as I had left it. Nothing seemed out of place, except the grass was a little long in the front. I would take care of that tomorrow and anything else that needed to be repaired or tended to. Closing my eyes I took a deep breath letting Earth's air settle in my lungs. Everything here was different from the bustling city of Ozryn. I didn't have to worry about running into another Shadow Assassin; it was less noisy, leaving me to my thoughts. Just peace and quiet; I wondered how long that would last.

FOR THE NEXT FEW WEEKS, I took care of everything at home while simultaneously jumping in to check on the female whose name I had discovered was Raine. Such a beautiful name for a lovely female. She was blossoming and had spent a lot of time outdoors. Back on AshFiera, I had guessed as much, and it had never failed. Watching her run every morning and hitting those bags in the evenings. It was beautiful to gaze upon for hours on end, and I imagined what it would be like to run my hands down her arms and over her aching hands. Bringing them down her sides, grabbing her hips while I stood behind her. I wanted to pull her soft body to my hard one. Clearing my throat, I continued to study Raine until she went inside. I did this every day, and without fail, I would fantasize about finally getting my hands on her.

That was until one morning when she hadn't emerged from the house. It was past dinnertime when her Aunt came out the back door of their home, on the phone with someone. I eagerly listened to a one-sided conversation since I couldn't understand the person on the other end.

"Gage, what happened yesterday at the club? She hasn't come out of her room or eaten anything all day. It's so unlike her."

She chewed on her fingernail, listening to whatever this Gage person said, shaking her head.

"Oh no, poor Raine. I'm sure what happened is

destroying her inside." There was a worried wobble to her voice that told me it wasn't good, whatever she was hearing.

She made another brief pause before finishing the conversation. "Yes, I understand. I'll speak with her and let her know that Jen is going to make a full recovery in no time and that she doesn't blame her for what happened. It won't be easy to convince Raine, but we'll see. Okay, talk to you soon."

My heart ached for Raine; I wanted to be her shoulder to cry on and a body to wrap herself in with whatever happened. But I knew she didn't have knowledge of me, and I would have to wait for the opportune time to introduce myself.

So I waited and waited. Several more weeks went by, and Raine still hadn't left the house or her room. I was starting to go out of my mind. Not seeing her all these weeks drove something inside mad. I had sworn to myself that when I laid eyes on her next, I wouldn't hesitate. I would reveal myself. I would wrap her up inside my arms and chase away whatever darkness lay beneath her skin.

Goddess above, I loved her from afar and wanted to love her up close. She was my soul, the other half of me. My Enayah.

Lost in thought, I didn't realize anyone had opened the back patio door until I saw a female silhouette begin to run.

I stopped myself from going to her when my body wanted nothing more than to chase her down and ensure she was alright. The previous promise of revealing myself to her was forgotten as I lost myself in her presence. Deciding it was best to continue to safeguard her from afar for the time being, I made my way closer to her workout area, which had been constructed several weeks ago. I only wanted to be closer to her.

An hour or so had passed when she finally returned to the punching bags. She began to wail on them, and when she hit it so hard on her last punch that it flew a few feet into the grass.

A piercing scream left her, and those emotions buried themselves deep into my soul punching straight into my heart.

Something had shattered within her, but I witnessed the slow relief morph onto her face, with her eyes still closed. She wouldn't be devastated for long; when the time was right, I would help her piece it back together as much as she would allow me to.

My body unconsciously leaned toward her, instinctively drawing closer. That's when I stepped and snapped a branch. Growling at myself, Raine's gaze instantly looked in my direction. Frozen and unable to move with her piercing stare.

Could she see me in the darkness?

She had yelled something at me, but I was too busy looking around, trying to find anything to distract her. That's when I glimpsed at a rabbit rummaging around for food behind me; I shadow-jumped. Grabbing it quickly, and jumping back to the spot I had been. Letting it go, the rabbit ran out of the woods, and I looked up at Raine. Her body had been tense when I snapped that fucking branch, and now her body had visibly relaxed seeing the rabbit run out of the woods instead of a grown-ass male who couldn't keep quiet.

Angry with myself it was apparent I was easily distracted by this female. And I needed to be more vigilant, or someone would get hurt if something arose unexpectedly.

A moment later, a truck entered the driveway and stopped beside the house. An older male got out and approached Raine. I tensed, but it seemed she knew him. A moment later, I it had to be the male she liked to spar with on occasion. I hadn't recognized him at first without the gym clothes. He was dressed like he had somewhere special he was going.

Listening carefully to their conversation I found out a competition was going to happen at the club. *Interesting.* I wondered if I could gain enough trust to be invited. It would be cutting it close; two weeks wasn't long enough to acquaint myself with these males, but I would make it work. I had to introduce myself and budge my way into her life at some point anyway. It would be the perfect time to do it, too.

Chapter Seven
Raine

A lot happened in the last two weeks leading up to the 'friendly' but competitive match that was about to happen this weekend.

Gigi and Aunt Sam left on their cruise a few days ago. They could only make calls to check up on me when they were docked at a port. So, it's been primarily silent around the house.

The only noise around here was when I hit the bags, along with the occasional visit from Gage. He was still worried about me, and I kept insisting I was fine. I had spilled the beans and decided to join in on the fun that all the 'boys' would be involved in. He let me know that a few new members had recently joined the club as well. Checking to make sure I was okay with unknown men joining the group. I shrugged and told him, 'The more, the merrier.'

It was the night of the first fights. I chose to walk all the way to rid myself of the unsettling feelings I had all day leading up to the matches.

Making it to the club, I looked over the parking lot. It

was packed, more than it had ever been. *What the hell? Why are there so many people? I thought Gage said it was only going to be a small gathering.*

The questions swirled in my head, and then I spotted Gage. He was waving me over near the side door, so I stomped over to him with a searing glare that made him visibly wince.

Immediately, I laid into him, "What the fuck, Gage? What happened to it being something small? It's way too big." Pointing a finger out into the overflowing parking lot. People were starting to park on the road as I spoke with him.

"I know Raine. One of the guys, Mac, does promotional work and thought it would be a great idea for people to come out and cheer everyone on. We are hosting a charity event to raise funds for children in need. I didn't think it would bother you." Gage said sheepishly.

"A little warning next time would have been nice," I grumbled. "I don't mind, not if it's for something good." I paused, tapping a finger on my chin, thinking of ways I could get back at Mac, who I had spoken to several times over the last few weeks. "So, does this mean I secure the first chance to go up against Mac? Because I'm going to kick his ass for doing such a good job promoting tonight." I chuckled, my eyes lighting up, letting Gage comprehend I wasn't mad.

He nodded and opened the door further so I could enter the boxers' area.

Once inside, he brought me to a room with my name taped to the door. Turning, I raised an eyebrow. "Since you're the only woman competing, you're allowed a separate space from the guys," Gage said.

I was the *only* woman competing; I needed to remember that so I didn't go spiraling like I had after everything with

Jen. So, I was grateful they gave me the privilege of having a separate area. It was better than being in the locker room with all the guys. I needed the privacy to change into my outfit without others ogling me.

After a while, I was ready to go. The adrenaline rushed through my body when I walked into the central part of the building that held the large boxing ring. Looking around, I took in the tightly packed event. My eyes widened in awe at how many people were in attendance. Some of the guys had already started their fights with the other opponents in the ring, so I looked for a few of the other participants, including Mac. Spotting them near the concessions, I headed in that direction.

Getting closer, one of the guys noticed me walking toward them and hollered my name, making all the rest turn and start waving their arms frantically. It was comical to witness. It reminded me of a bunch of toddlers wanting attention or wanting 'uppies.'

Walking up to the group, I gave them a big grin, turning my attention and focusing on Mac, "You and me. I'm challenging you first since you neglected to mention anything about all this." I swept my hand around the packed club. "I had decided I wanted to beat all your asses for some burgers since that's what Gage promised. So I'm here to join after all."

Mac smirked back at me, "I absolutely accept this challenge from you, Raine. And you bet your ass there will be burgers. I got Burgers N' More to sponsor the fights tonight and tomorrow. They are providing all the fighters with free burgers and fries."

"Stop! Oh, my Goddess Mac. I might love you." I said jokingly with a hand placed over my heart. "But, I still intend to kick your ass along with any of the guys here who want to take on little ole me."

"Little lady, you'd better be prepared to eat your words." Another one of the guys chuckled.

"See you boys out in the ring. I can't make any promises, but I'll attempt to be gentle," I said, swaying my hips and walking away to grab the rest of my gear and ready myself to fight Mac. I heard a whistle, and then the men laughed as I flipped them off without looking back.

THE FIGHT with Mac was just about to begin when tingling began creeping up my neck, goosebumps rapidly spreading down my arms. Looking around the building, I couldn't decipher who it was; too many eyes were already on me since I was currently the center of attention while standing in the middle of the ring with Mac.

Ding, Ding. Snapping my attention back to the man who put all this together as he approached. His eyes shone with concern for a moment. "You okay, Raine?" He asked.

"Yeah, I'm good." I replied, before taunting him. "You okay? Seeing as I am going to beat you in, oh let's say, less than five minutes from now?" I said. Grinning when his eyes widened and his laugh boomed over the already rowdy audience.

He didn't wait any longer and struck. Tackling my body and slamming my back to the mat, his hands gripping my thighs. He nestled his large frame in between my legs, so I took that opportunity to wrap my legs around his back while slinging my arms around his neck. Tucking his face into my chest, I huffed another taunt into his ear, "You ready to tap out, Mac?"

"No way, I haven't even broken a sweat yet, sweets." He muffled. His face was still squished against my body.

"Don't say I didn't warn you, dude."

The vibrations of his laughter rolled over my body, and I grinned when his grip on my thighs loosened.

Taking the opportunity, I squeezed the upper half of my body out from under him and draped myself across his back. The position let me further swing my legs around allowing me to be a human backpack.

Wrapping my arm back around Mac's throat, I tightened the hold I had on him. The grunt was the first sound he made, and it was music to my ears. Mac fell backward with my body still hanging on tight. The thud and impact of the ground with his bulky momentum left me gritting my teeth, but I had him.

The fight with Mac didn't last much longer. He conceded rather quickly, tapping out on my arm when he could no longer breathe, and I was named the winner. It only made the other men more eager to go against me. So, one by one, they went down, making the crowd go wild. I beat three more guys after Mac when I called it quits for the night–exhausted, sore, and hungry.

Eyeing the burger table, I marched quickly to it and scooped up several burgers and a big heaping pile of fries while I had a separate container that held an obscene amount of ketchup. I had been addicted to the red, thick, and pasty goodness ever since Aunt Sam first took me to the burger joint sponsoring the fights.

She made fun of me the first time I had it. Telling me it was weird to take a spoon and eat the ketchup alone. I couldn't help it; it was too good, and it complemented the burgers and fries well, so I used the food to scoop big globs into my mouth instead.

I was finishing eating when I felt another bout of tingling, crawling slowly up my back and neck. There was no mistaking it; I continued to experience these episodes of being watched several times. First, at the falls before I left AshFiera, and then for the first few weeks, I was on Earth, more specifically when I was outside of Gigi and Sam's home. I had called out to the feeling in the past, but I was always left with no response. As more time passed, I grew accustomed to the feeling. When I holed myself up in my room for those couple of weeks after the accident, I didn't feel it.

Whoever it was had been watching me while I was outside. But now, they were in the building somewhere— they could be anywhere. And I couldn't tell where it was coming from. Too many people were looking my way again. My face was now familiar and popular after going unde-feated tonight. It was hard to tell where it originated, but it was becoming so familiar. It made goosebumps move up my arms each time.

I gathered my belongings after throwing away my plates and made my way to the door. Gage stopped me as I was about to exit.

"Raine, let me give you a ride home tonight. It's too late for you to walk back, and you have a busy day tomorrow."

"That would be great, Gage, thank you! And why do I have a busy day tomorrow?" I asked, suspicion edging my voice.

"Well, there is a lineup of guys who want to try to defeat you. They caught a glimpse of your skills tonight, and their egos are at an all-time high, thinking they can beat you." He smirked and shrugged.

"Yeah, but Gage, it's not exactly a fight when all they do is tackle me to the ground. They don't even try to hit me. They should know I'm not fragile." I pointed out.

"I think they don't want to mar that beautiful face. It's easier for them to pin you and think they can win against you that way. Since you are smaller than them." He responded.

"But they didn't win." I chuckled. "I end up wiggling my way out of their hold, wrapping my body around their backs, and throwing my arm around their throats. When I do that move, they give up real quick, though. I think it's my new favorite." I said proudly. Which was true, it was pretty fun putting the guys I had grown to know in their place.

"Huh, it is a great move." Silence wrapped around us as we headed out of the building, to his truck.

Most of the ride was quiet until we pulled up the driveway, and Gage parked. He spoke as I got out, "I am proud of you, kiddo. For leaving the house and coming out tonight. I think it's good not to be cooped up and hidden away for that long."

"I appreciate the push, Gage. But uh, can you leave the sappy shit for my Aunt? Hearing you be sweet to me and not push my buttons is too weird." I said, smiling at him.

"Got it, kiddo. I miss your Aunt, too, by the way. I can't wait for her to be home in a couple of weeks. Anyway, see you tomorrow." Gage said, putting the truck into gear before I backed away.

"Later," I said, waving to him as I sprinted up the steps into the house.

I was thinking about Gigi and Aunt Sam, away on their cruise, having fun, and it left me happy. They insisted they stay behind, not wanting me to be left alone, knowing I had assassins scouring AshFiera and maybe even here on Earth.

I told them that they were not going to cancel a trip they had been planning for years. Their plans had long been in motion before I dropped into their laps. It was expensive since it was a month-long endeavor. And then, when I wouldn't budge, they insisted that Gage stay with me, but I put a stop to that as well. I was an adult, not some child who needed a babysitter.

Looking at the clock, I realized it was getting far too late, and if I didn't close my eyes and sleep, I would pay dearly for it in the morning.

It didn't take long to pass out. My body exhausted from the day's exertions, I let myself dive into darkness.

WAKING up the next morning sore, I spotted a bruise that was beginning to form on my left hip. I didn't have knowledge of how many men decided they wanted a chance to go against me today. Gage wasn't very open about it. My body would likely work harder today, that was a real possibility, and I would likely have more bruises.

Making sure to eat a large protein-based breakfast, I primed myself for the walk to the club.

The evening hit quickly as the day blurred past me. I was still undefeated and demolished another four big beef-cakes. They were all steroids and hardly any real strength behind them. Of course, as predicted, every one of them wrestled me to the mat. And I got out of it quickly. They underestimated my more petite, lithe body than theirs. It was a lot of fun, though, and I was having the time of my life.

I tapped myself out of any more 'fights' for the evening.

Starving again, I grabbed even more burgers and fries with my ketchup hoard. I sat at the table, watching the other guys go at each other in the ring.

Mac and Gage had declared me the winner long ago. Now it was just a pissing match for them. They were trying to win back those bruised egos.

As I shoved a giant, juicy burger into my mouth, Gage and Mac walked up to where I was relaxing. Big smiles spread on both their faces.

"Can I help you two cheshires out?" I tried asking, chewing around a large bite of a burger.

Gage stood there smiling while Mac started, "Raine, I need you to listen to us. Don't say anything yet because this is huge. There's a guy who joined the club a few weeks ago and has contributed so much to the club already."

Gage cut in excitely, "He wants to fight you."

"Hush, let me finish my thoughts, let's build into it first." Mac glared at him. "So, he has been a great addition to the club. Teaching some of the guys mixed martial arts."

I cut him off this time, "So you're telling me the guys who I have been tackled by the last two nights are using a different technique to try to beat me? And this new guy taught them?"

"Uh, yeah. I suppose that's what was happening. He's great, though, I promise. He said if you agreed, he would donate fifty grand to the kids' charities!" Mac said excitely.

With the burger poised in my mouth, ready to bite down, I stopped the movement and looked up. My eyes widened, first glancing at Gage and then at Mac. I dropped my burger on the plate.

Whistling low, I answered, "Fifty pops, huh? That's ridiculous. Have you met the guy? I bet he's crazy, isn't he? 'Cause that's an absurd amount to drop." I sat back and blew out a breath, thinking momentarily. "Alright, screw it, I'm in. But! You guys owe me so many fucking burgers and fries after this is done. And I don't mean tonight either, since you both rudely interrupted a girl and her feast. You'll both owe me for a long time. You're my burger bitches now." I smiled menacingly.

"Let me tell him you're in. We will give you an hour to settle your stomach, since you've already pounded two burgers away. We don't need you getting sick in the ring," Gage said, walking away to find this mystery man.

Mac didn't linger long, either. He needed to announce that a huge fight was being arranged in exchange for a large sum donation.

An hour and a long walk later, it was time to kick some ass and take his name. Or, however, that human saying went.

Walking into the event center, loud cheers erupted as the crowd discovered my arrival. I waved and jumped right up into the ring.

Mac's voice boomed over the speakers, "First up, you all know her as the undefeated Queen of the Ring, but we know her as Raine!" The crowd went wild, and I waved more, grinning from ear to ear. "Next, we have our largest benefactor. Coming in and donating an extravagant amount of fifty thousand dollars. All so he could have a chance to steal her undefeated title. May I present to you, 'The Prince of Darkness,' Kal!"

Giggling at Mac's dramatics, I turned to face my opponent and gasped. *Holy fuckery. Who is this specimen, and why is he so delicious? Oh boy, I am in trouble.*

Staring at the man in front of me. I took in the shadow he cast on the mat that had to be twice the size of mine. His broad shoulders led to deliciously thick arms. If I were to try and wrap both my hands around his bicep, there would be no way my fingers would touch. He was shirtless, which gave me a great view of his ink. Across his chest, a mural of stars was scattered. They looked oddly like the ones from back home. That couldn't be right, though. It had to be a coincidence that he mapped out the stars like that.

Bemused, my gaze slowly rose. Craning my neck to look back up at his face. He had a devilish grin, which made my heart pound hard and my insides heat. A neatly trimmed beard matched the color of his inky black hair. I had to admit I was a sucker for a man with facial hair. My eyes kept trailing up to his, where they locked onto mine. His irises were like swirls of golden honey, perfectly matching the highlights in my hair. I was being pulled right in by those unnaturally bright orbs. He was distracting, to say the least, when his fingers started running through the top of his hair. I pictured it being my fingers rubbing along the short sides. And then gliding them up as I slid them to his longer top, grabbing and bringing his lush lips closer to mine for a kiss.

Shaking my head clear, I stepped back. *Bad girl, Raine. Get a hold of yourself, you fucking feen. Focus and kick this incredibly handsome man's ass so you can return to your juicy burgers.*

"You both agree to the rules? It's a friendly fight, have fun, and don't kick each other's asses too much." Gage said near us.

Nodding, we took our positions and waited for the bell to sound, indicating the start of the round. It wasn't long before it went off.

I started circling Kal, gauging the best outcome for a win. The other guys made it easy when they went straight to tackling, but Kal didn't follow suit. Instead, he circled with me.

My patience was wearing thin; I had more burgers to devour. So I struck first and made a punch to his waist. Motherfucker didn't even flinch. But I was close enough to him now that he made his move. He pushed me into the netting wall and hooked one arm over my shoulder while the other one went between my legs. He lifted my body and then gently placed me on the mat while being pinned.

Stunned, it took me a few seconds to realize he wasn't holding me tight. So I wiggled my way free, bucking him off, causing him to fall backward onto his ass. I launched myself at him, pushing him down and straddling his hips as I leaned my body forward and applied pressure to his throat with my forearm.

He smiled like the cocky man that he was and gripped onto my hips, squeezing slightly, causing my core to tingle and my cheeks to heat. He flipped me onto my back and wedged his thick body between my thighs. I was breathing heavily, my nostrils flaring, glaring at him.

My body was heating up in more ways than one. The air was charged with sexual tension as Kal tried pinning my legs tightly to my body, leaving my arms free. So I maneuvered myself using those arms to my advantage and out of his hold, climbing onto his back. I wrapped both arms around his neck and squeezed again. I chose not to be gentle with him like he had been with me earlier. I meant business and wanted this over quickly. He lasted longer in the ring than anyone else, and I was tiring out fast.

I almost gave up until I felt his shift, and he tapped out on my arm. Letting go, I stood up, and Gage grabbed my arm. Mac raised the other while he announced my undefeated win over the loudspeakers.

Beaming with joy, I looked over at Kal. He smiled back at me and spoke for the first time, "Congratulations, Raine. You fought beautifully." His voice was deep and rich. I could feel the bass rumble through my body, causing more pulsing in my core.

"Thanks, Kal, you're not so bad yourself," I said, walking away. I needed some distance from whatever was running through my body and the reaction to being in Kal's presence.

Fresh burgers and fries were calling my name, and I was not letting anything or anyone stand in my way. Not even the irresistibly sexy man I left behind at the ring.

After shoving my face full of goodness, I stuck around to watch the other guys go at each other. It was still remarkably packed here, so I didn't pay attention when someone new sat beside me until the electricity in the air charged again.

Turning my head, I gazed over at Kal, who intently watched the crowd, turning his head he focused on me. "Heeey." I drawled out, "What brings you to the neighborhood?"

He gave me a crooked smile, "Oh, you know, watching some fights. I got my ass kicked by a female, and now I have to lick my wounds."

"Female, huh? Well, she must be a badass bitch to take on such a big baby." I laughed out, loudly causing some of the bystanders to glance over at us.

"She is indeed." He turned his body towards me, giving me his full attention, "I would very much like to gain the honor of learning about you, Raine. May I take you home?"

"Slow it down, there, tiger. Stick around the club. I'm sure we will learn more about each other, like I did with the other delinquent men here." I looked away from him; his gaze was so intense it made me want to squirm in my seat. "As far as taking me home. I enjoy walking; it helps clear my mind. So I'm going to have to decline. Plus, I don't sleep with men that I just met."

"Hold on now, I wasn't asking to take you home to sleep with you. It's dark, and I wouldn't want a stranger to run up on you." Kal said, making sure to let me know he was a gentleman and not someone wanting in my panties. Too bad because if I had gotten to know him sooner, I would have certainly entertained the idea.

"Oh–well, that's good to know. But you do realize I can handle myself? I kicked five men's asses tonight. Which includes you, by the way." I said, poking a finger into his buff arm. I couldn't resist touching him. It was too tempting, he was too irresistible.

"Point made. Perhaps you'll see me around, Raine. Have a glorious walk home." His smile widened, showing off fangs, and then he got up, walking away.

My brows furrowed, and my gaze stuck to his back as I watched him walk out the door. Most humans didn't have fangs. It was possible but scarce. Who the heck was this man? Why did I have such a reaction from him? And would I see him again—soon?

There were so many unanswered questions. I needed to clear them. The night wasn't over for most of the men, but my eyes drooped and the social meter ran out. Finding Gage, I used my hands to signal I was headed home and ended it with a peace-out sign. Tilting my head back and laughing when he looked confused, shrugging, and then returning to talking with the patrons.

When I finally walked up the driveway to the house, it was late. My mind kept going back to Kal and our fight. It felt incredibly intimate and left me breathless. His hands on my hips left trails of fire lighting up in my veins.

Thinking about him left my body aching for his touch again. Clearing my throat and shaking my head to clear it, I decided to look up at the stars. "I miss you so much, Mom. I wish you could have been there to see me tonight. I wish you could just be here with me."

Wetness fell down my cheek, and I closed my eyes. Taking a deep breath, I slowly exhaled, taking the moment to ground myself. Then I snapped my head up, looking around at my surroundings.

Nothing but pitch black greeted me, but it was there again. It felt less frightening tonight, like a familiar and comforting caress against my face.

Someone was there again, had to be, beyond the woods.

I didn't linger much longer in the unknown presence; I opened the front door and entered. Closing it tightly behind me, I left the stranger to lurk in the shadows.

Chapter Eight
Kal

Two weeks prior to the fights.

After discovering that competitive fights were happening, I left Raine's. Materializing near the club so I wouldn't draw attention to myself. I walked through the parking lot and up to the building. It was a massive facility; across the front was a large sign that said The MoonBright with a moon hidden behind its words. There were several doors dotted along the sides of the building, but I was aiming for the large double doors in front.

Various machines inside were occupied by several individuals, with a group of males standing next to a couple of them. One looked to be speaking with the group in an animated manner.

He spotted me while I was looking around. "Hey! Bud, over here!" He said, waving one hand above his head.

Walking over to the group, I realized this could be easier than I thought. The humans seemed friendly and invited anyone over to their discussion.

"Hey, man, name's Mac. I help run MoonBright while the owner is out. What can I help ya with?" the male asked.

"Just looking for a place to let some steam loose. And meet new people while I'm in town." I said.

"Great! We're all friends here. We were talking about an upcoming event I am hosting in the back of the building. It's in a few weeks. And all of us will be fighting each other for a chance to claim bragging rights. I'm also setting it up as a charity." Mac said, being quite open with his plans.

I knew there was a competition, and this was my opening. "Sounds great, Mac. Are you letting anyone join?" I inquired. "I would love to help out any way I can." I paused to look at him, "When the time comes, I can donate. And in the meantime, if anyone's interested, I can teach them mixed martial arts." I shrugged nonchalantly, "It's a more interesting fighting style that I like."

"Hold up! You would be willing to teach us a better way to fight?" someone in the back said.

"A better way? Isn't the way you fight now not good enough?" I inquired, wondering what they meant.

Mac spoke up to answer, "The guys want an advantage. There's a woman who will hopefully be joining. She's hell-a-strong and can drop a guy in seconds. Gage, the owner, is dating her aunt, so she often comes in. The guys like goading her. She recently took a break, and Gage headed out to her place to encourage her to join us."

Bingo, I found my way in. This was definitely much easier than I thought it would be.

"I might have to challenge her myself and scope out if she's truly strong or if you guys are being nice to earn her favor."

Mac laughed, "Yeah, the guys don't play nice when it comes to her. She's fantastic and a hard worker; just wait and see."

I didn't need to see. I was already watching Raine at home; she just didn't know it yet.

And I would continue to do so for the next two weeks.

I split my time between teaching the guys new moves, earning their trust, and then watching over Raine in the evenings. I admired how she moved with ease, never missing a step and keeping in time with whatever beats were playing on the radio she had on.

It was addicting being her guardian. I hoped she would allow me to be her shield in every aspect when she finally met me.

The first night of the fights, I sat back and enjoyed watching Raine. She was marvelous. Mac had his ass handed to him quickly, and I gave him shit for it afterward. I ensured she wasn't around when I spoke with any of the guys. I wasn't ready for her to meet me yet.

I only fought the guys in the ring when she went out of sight to rest in her room. She could feel my presence, though. I was sure it was beginning to feel familiar.

But was it a comfort to know she was being watched? Or was I a fool for becoming so obsessed with her and making her uncomfortable?

I couldn't help it. The female's scent drove an innate part of me crazy with need. I would have to be careful when I fought her, making sure my desire was hidden. I didn't want to embarrass myself in front of her and look like a fool.

IT WAS the evening of the second night, and Raine had finished her latest win. I found Mac near the food tables designated for the fighters. "Mac, I have a proposition for you regarding Raine's next fight."

He cocked an eyebrow, "She's starting to get tired, Kal. I don't think she has anything left in her. She kept eyeing the food tables, and I heard her stomach growl before the last round. Can't come between a woman and her food."

"What if I made it good? I'll donate fifty grand towards the charity in exchange for her last fight. I'll even go easy on her." I said with a smirk.

"What?!? Holy shit, that's double what we have raised in the last two nights."

"I understand that, just imagine the crowd will go wild if you announce it, and will go even crazier if she wins," I said, anticipating that I would likely let her win regardless.

"I don't think you need to let her win, man. I guarantee she will kick your ass on her own. She's been on fire tonight." Mac placated.

I grunted in response, "Huh—yeah, we will see about that."

"Alright, I'm running to find Gage, and both of us will break it to her, saying that she will have to hold off on eating for one more round." He said, taking off in a run toward where Gage was standing.

It didn't take long, and he returned to inform me that I would fight Raine in an hour. She had already been eating when they approached her, so her stomach needed time to settle.

An hour later, the match with Raine started. We circled each other, and she lost her patience. Lunging forward, she aimed for my stomach. When she hit, it felt like she had the strength of a female Shadow Assassin. I internally cringed. My face was a blank slate; I was trying not to show that it affected me as much as it did.

She was closer to me now, and I moved, grabbing her and pinning her to the floor. I made sure the impact was directed at my arms, not wanting to injure her purposely.

My nose was close to her neck, and I took in a big inhale. The jasmine and honey went straight to my cock, and it started to harden. Before I knew it, she got herself free and knocked me on my ass. Tackling me to the floor of the ring, I felt her legs on both sides of my hips and her arm at my throat.

Oh, this was not good. I need to get out of this.

If she shifted the right way, she would feel my half-hard erection, and it would likely harden further if she rubbed herself against it.

Gripping those delicious hips, I flipped her onto her back. I was still between her legs, but I could control how close I was to the apex of her thighs.

Pushing her legs closer to her body, I wanted her to tap out. I wanted to preen and boast that I was a better male than the rest, show her I was strong and could protect her. But what little strength she had left, she used to slip her way behind my back.

Using an arm, she wrapped it around my neck. I had to let go of her legs, and she took advantage of the opportunity. With all her weight and strength bearing down on my neck, black spots began to dot my vision. So, I did the only logical thing to avoid hurting my female. I tapped out on her arm before I lost consciousness and trapped her beneath my heavy body. Immediately, she let go and took a step back.

The crowd was going wild. I congratulated Raine and left the ring, watching her victory from afar. She had only one thing on her mind afterward, and it was food, so I left her alone, only interrupting later on to ask her if she needed a ride. She was a visionary with a quick-witted tongue, insinuating I wanted to sleep with her, which I most certainly did, but I needed her to trust me. And get home safe.

I left before her, taking the same route she would. Making sure it was clear of any dangers, and then took up my spot in the trees guarding her home. It was not long before she was walking up the driveway, stopping briefly to look up at the stars and speak with her dead mother.

The shift in her demeanor was slight, but she knew I was there watching. She still didn't know it was me, but soon she would find out who lurked in the shadows, guarding her.

I AWOKE WITH A START, looking at my clock. It read three in the morning. I didn't know what woke me from my slumber, but something felt off.

Getting dressed quickly, I made sure to grab my weapons and prepared to jump to Raine's. The feeling intensified as the moments ticked by.

Shadow-jumping to my hideout, I scanned the area.

Nothing seemed out of the ordinary until I spotted Raine climbing out of her window. Luckily, her bedroom was on the first story, so she had a very short fall.

She was running barefoot in a nightgown, headed right for me. Just before she made it to where I hid, she was almost taken out by an arrow that shot past her.

Tackling her to the ground, I spotted another male knocking an arrow, aiming in our direction.

Her eyes were round, staring up at me. "What the fuck– Kal? A-are you stalking me? How the hell did you know where I lived?"

"One thing at a time, my little Enayah. But yes, I have been keeping guard over you." I said, looking up and calculating how long I had until one of them reached us.

When I saved Raine, we rolled out of view, and I could decipher at least two Shadow Assassins talking to each other.

"What did you call me? And I don't think 'keeping guard' is what I would classify stalking as, you creep." She hissed at me.

I grunted, ignoring what she said, and then I was on the move. One second, I was on top of the alluring female, and then the next, I shadow-jumped to the first assailant I found. He seemed surprised to see another assassin. And he wasn't quick enough before my dagger sliced his throat. The other assassin's eyes widened, and he disappeared.

Shit, well, can't kill that one yet.

I didn't have time to go after him. I needed to find Raine and make sure she was still safe.

Glancing back to where I had left her, my eyes scanned an empty indent in the leaves where she had been lying. My heart thudded violently in my chest.

Where the hell did she run to?

Looking back over her home, I didn't spot any movement. There was no thumping of footsteps or running nearby, so I inhaled deeply. Catching her scent on the wind in the opposite direction of the house. I had to ensure that no one followed her after she took off while I was busy. So I followed her scent through the woods until I came upon a cave.

I listened for a moment and could pick up her shuffling.

She was safe. So, I would sit here for however long and wait for her to emerge on her own. I didn't want to startle her any further than she had been from the events that just took place.

I might have been in for a wait, but I would sit here however long it took for her to leave the safety of the cave.

Chapter Nine
Raine

My eyes lazily opened. It was still dark out. Comfortably lying in bed, looking at the ceiling with blurry eyes, wondering why I was awake.

Rubbing the lids softly, I turned my head to look for my phone. Turning on the screen, my eyes blinked rapidly, trying to focus on the blinding light.

Two-Fifty-Five. Shit, it's way too early.

Lying back down in the soft covers, I closed my eyes, willing my body to fall back to sleep. The seconds ticked by, and I frustratingly sat up in bed and rubbed my face.

One of Gigi's vases in the other room shattered, and a moment later, a thud reverberated, and shortly after that, a second boom indicated there was more going on.

Crawling out of bed, I slowly opened my door and quietly crept down the hall to peer around the wall where the living room was.

My eyes widened as they landed on two huge men who were in the middle of the room. No–these weren't men from Earth, but males from AshFiera.

Fuck, the assassin's found me.

A third thump sounded with a grunt. I didn't stick around to witness who else joined the group of males. I was far outnumbered.

Sneaking back to my room, I closed the door behind me, leaning a chair against the handle. I didn't know if that would hold them—not if the assassins tried checking this room. The males of AshFiera had wicked good noses, and I wanted as much of a head start as possible. I had no time to change out of my nightgown, and my shoes were left by the front door.

Grabbing the window, I unlocked it slowly, inching it upward to climb out.

I had to make it to the forest without being seen or heard. Then, I would run to the cave I found weeks ago while hiking. I would hide out until they lost interest in finding me or until the sun rose so I could see where I was headed.

The door handle jiggled as I was halfway out the window. And as the last of my body slipped out, I looked back when the door splintered open. Briefly, I set my eyes on Patches in the doorway, glaring at me before I turned around and took off.

That cocky motherfucker is here. I should have known he would come for me.

Running across the lawn into the dark woods, my feet slipped in the morning dew coating the grass. I was reaching the tree line when I heard a whiz rush past my ear, and then I was suddenly tackled to the ground.

"Oof," A massive body had wedged between my legs, and when I looked up at who it was, my eyes widened, "What the fuck—Kal? A-are you stalking me? How the hell did you know where I lived?"

103

He gave me a dazzling grin that took my breath away. "One thing at a time, my little Enayah. But, yes, I was keeping guard over you." He said, looking away from me and to the house. I tried tilting my head to catch what he was looking at, but what he called me threw me off.

The fuck did he say? Did I hear that correctly?

Because that sounded more like stalking than 'guarding', especially if I didn't know he was there. It made me want to punch him in his perfectly handsome face. "What did you call me? And I don't think 'keeping guard' is what I would classify stalking as, you creep."

Kal grunted, indicating he heard but ignoring me all the same. One second, he was on top of me, a heavy weight that felt unnecessarily right between my thighs. And then the next, he disappeared from above my body.

Rolling onto my stomach, I looked over the lawn where Kal suddenly appeared. I followed his movements while he sliced his dagger across the assassin's throat.

I had just met Kal tonight. I didn't understand what he wanted with me. And I wasn't going to stick around to find out, either. Knowing he certainly wasn't human or a warlock from Earth, I didn't feel safe anymore. So I ran.

I ran so hard that I barely realized I had collected scrapes along my legs and feet from the low-lying bushes. I only slowed down when a branch smacked me in the face, leaving a welt on my left cheek under my eye, narrowly missing it.

After running for so long and spotting the cave ahead, it was like a beacon shining in the dark for a lost ship at sea.

As I approached the cave, the dull throb in the soles of my feet started pounding in time with my heartbeat, and I knew I wouldn't be going any further tonight. Hesitantly, I looked over my shoulder. I couldn't see far in the dark, but I knew I was alone. And I hoped it would stay that way.

I had to wait until after sunrise. Then, I would need to figure out how to obtain better clothing and some food. I wasn't hungry yet, but I wasn't a fool. I knew I wouldn't last long without the basic survival needs being met.

Returning home to Gigi and Aunt Samara's wasn't an option now. The assassins knew where I lived, and I had no idea if they would put a scout in place to keep guard for my return. I hoped Gigi and Aunt Sam wouldn't call my phone anytime soon, either. Or Gage. I didn't want them to return to the house early if I didn't answer, and end up hurt because of me.

An uncontrollable sob left my throat. My life was upended yet again.

Would I ever be free? Would they ever stop chasing me? Is this what my life was now? Being chased and having to run every time because I wasn't confident enough in my ability to handle combat.

I felt like a failure again. I was failing my mom and myself. Shaking my head and hands, I exhaled and entered the cave, my safe haven.

When I limped inside, it was cold and damp. The cave was crisp and cool near the entrance, and it began to warm up as I approached the back, where a small pool with steam rising from the water was located. I sighed and plopped down at the edge, draping my legs over to submerge them and my feet in the hot water.

Keeping my feet in the heated wetness, I laid on my back and looked up at the cave's ceiling. I smiled when the blue lights brightened while I lay still on the ground. I regarded them, and they started to flicker, my body relaxing even though the ground beneath me was hard.

I wasn't sure how long I had been in the cave, soaking my legs and feet, staring up at the bioluminescent organisms above me, that was, until the sun started peering into the cave entrance. It was time to go. I needed to find help. Surely the club would be open. I could walk to the gym, and one of the guys would call Gage to help me. It would take longer than I wanted, but I had to do it; I had no one else I trusted in this world who was close enough.

After getting to my feet, I slowly started walking to the entrance, getting accustomed to the prickling sensation that intensified every time I put pressure on them.

I hissed, grabbed hold of the wall, and then screamed as a shadow blocked most of the sunlight. The male placed a hand over my mouth as he grabbed my body to help me steady. I threw an elbow into what I hoped was my assailant's side. But he was too quick, grabbing my arm and securing it behind my back and then pushing me against the cave wall. Slowly, my eyes adjusted, and I realized it was Kal. He removed his hand from my mouth when I no longer screamed or tried fighting my way out of his hold. My body relaxed into his, only to stiffen again when I remembered he was stalking me.

"Get your hands off me, Kal." I started pushing at his chest when I realized he had let go of my arms.

"No, I'm helping you. Seeing as you hurt yourself while running from me." He stated the obvious.

Such an insufferable male.

"Of course, I'm going to run from you. I just met you last night, and you have been watching me like a lunatic!" I shouted at him, still trying to push out of his hold while trying to smack him in the face.

He guffawed at me and then gripped both wrists in his hand while placing them above my head, "We're back to this, are we? I was asked by a friend to keep an eye on you. This person knew something was going to happen to you. And they wanted me to be around to make sure you were kept safe."

He still held onto my wrists with one hand, but pushed his body into mine so he could brush a knuckle across my cheek.

Softly, he murmured, "And I have been ensuring you have been safe, my Enayah. I regarded you from afar, blossoming into someone stronger even after losing someone you love. I'm not sorry for that."

Leaning into him, I took a deep breath. He smelled like patchouli and sandalwood. The sweetly spiced, earthy tones imprinted on my soul the longer I took them in. I wanted to pull my wrists away to resist him, but my body refused to move. He drew me in, his body pulling an invisible thread to make me comply.

How could I feel safe with someone I just met? I had never been held like this by another man–male before. It felt nice. I let myself enjoy the hold only for a moment longer as a shiver ran down my spine, and I felt the goosebumps rise on my arms.

Clearing my throat, I spoke up, "I–um. Thanks, I guess?"

"No need to thank me; it has been my pleasure." He said, grinning down at me.

When he saw I was no longer fighting him, he let go of my wrists but refused to pull his body away. Instead, he loomed over me like he could shield me with his own body.

"So, I need to retrieve some clothes. I don't think I can go back home, though. Someone should be able to help me at the club. Can you help me get there?" I asked. Hoping I could at least have some sort of protection until I could get hold of Gage.

He nodded, "You look delectable in this gown, and though it pains me to see you in anything else. I agree you do need more clothing. However, I won't be bringing you to the club."

His declaration surprised me. "Excuse me?" Leaning away, I blinked up at him, confused why he would help but only in partial.

"If you will allow me to. I can take you back to my place, where I have clothes, a warm place to hide, and food. We can figure out what to do next from the comfort of my home."

It sounded logical. Kal was–at the moment–my only hope of getting out of this mess. One, I hadn't contemplated how to get out by myself. And the more I thought about it, the more it sounded better to go with him instead of putting Gage in harm's way.

Reluctantly, I said, "Alright, I agree to come with you. But! If you so much as make a move to screw me over, I'm kicking your ass again."

"You only kicked my ass because I was distracted last time, Enayah." He said, trying to play it cool, when I knew he didn't go easy on me. I barely won as it was, but I certainly did beat him.

I stared at him briefly, trying to figure out what it was he called me, "What does Enayah mean? You keep calling me that, and it's not familiar."

"If I don't tell you, you'll keep asking me, won't you?"

I shrugged. I likely wouldn't stop asking, especially if Kal continued to call me by that name. He stepped back from my body slightly but continued to hold onto my waist like it pained him to be far.

"It is the name of a rare star in the skies of AshFiera. It is a little like you, burning brightly but only when the sky's alight with dancing colors called an Elouven. Otherwise, on nights when it is dark, it is almost non-existent to the naked eye, hiding in plain sight. Something about the activity in the sky makes it come to life. Just like you, when you fight, it represents the dancing, and you brighten when you're in your element."

"Wow, that sounds so beautiful, but that was super cheesy too," I laughed. "Are you always so poetic?" I asked, rolling my eyes.

"Only with you," He paused, looking over his shoulder momentarily. "Raine, I need you to trust me. I understand it's a lot to ask, but we need to leave and be somewhere else. Away from your home. I'm afraid I only took out one of two assassins."

"Three. Three of them appeared in the house before I fled," I interrupted.

"Ah, well, it's even more imperative that I ask you to trust me now. The fastest way to travel to my home is to shadow-jump. Have you ever done it before?" He was staring into my eyes, waiting for my answer, and the sincerity in them helped ease the further tension that had been straining between us.

"No. My father said he wasn't allowed to jump with Mom or me. He had explained that he was only allowed to use it if his assignments required it." I said, repeating what my father had explained long ago, every time I had excitedly asked to come with him.

"Interesting, he was correct that he wasn't allowed to jump with anyone. However, they relaxed that rule long ago, allowing assassins to jump with close loved ones." Kal explained, leaving a question on my tongue. I didn't know who to ask because the one person I would have asked was Uncle Cass.

My stomach growled loudly, interrupting us and my thoughts.

"Let's get some food in you. I can't imagine how much louder your stomach will get if we ignore it. We don't want to alert anyone that we are here." Kal tried teasing, but my nerves were fried from what had happened, and irritation surfaced.

"Well, sorry, 'Captain Obvious,' I woke up in the middle of the night. Chased out of my home with nothing but a thin nightgown and hope." I paused. "Hope that I would make it out alive, like I had when I fled from my home in AshFiera."

"Raine–shit. I'm sorry, that was insensitive." He ran his fingers through his hair to smooth it back. "We'll go to my place to rest and eat. I'll contact my friend to find out if he has any insight into who is behind this. And go from there."

"Yeah–okay," I said, nodding, swiping a stray tear that had escaped, hoping he didn't catch the wetness on my cheek. "We can do that. I need to trust someone, and well, you're the only one here, I suppose."

"Since this is your first jump, I'll tell you what might happen. You might end up dizzy, but it shouldn't last long," the breathtakingly handsome Shadow Assassin explained. While I tried focusing on what he said, I couldn't help but be drawn to him the longer I was in his presence.

"I'm ready. Let's do this." I nodded. I could handle slight dizziness. No big deal–right?

I stepped further into his body and wrapped my arms around his neck, waiting for the sensations to begin. Before we dissolved into nothing, I felt his hand grip my hips, digging his fingers into my flesh. The gasp rolled off my tongue, left behind when darkness consumed us.

Chapter Ten
Raine

Kal and I disappeared, leaving the cave behind, reappearing in front of a beautiful home. I didn't have time to appreciate it much at the moment, as my vision blurred. If Kal hadn't already held onto my body, I would have fallen over into the freshly cut grass when the dizziness hit me.

What seemed like forever were only moments before my eyesight began to clear, and the spinning slowly dissipated.

I looked at our surroundings. The house was protected by a circle of pines that shielded it from the road, which was a few hundred feet away. It was a well-maintained property, as if someone had just trimmed the purple and blue floral bushes lined along the front and sides of the wrap-around porch. My gaze was drawn to the steps near the front door, where a swing hung from the ceiling. I wanted to sit on it with a blanket wrapped around my body. I wanted to watch the stars creep by in the sky. It looked peaceful and felt like a home.

That peace didn't last long, however. Kal tensed next to

me; his helpful arms, which had been wrapped around my body a moment before, disappeared, and I stumbled at the lost contact. A few crashes inside the house, followed by some grunts, told me an altercation was happening, and I was helpless, as I couldn't run, let alone walk, to the house. However, I didn't have to wait long as the door was abruptly ripped open while Kal and another male left the porch entangled together.

I intensely watched them go at each other, finally recognizing the other male.

"Uncle Cass?" I screeched, "Kal, stop! I know him. He's my mother's best friend and, for all intents and purposes, my Uncle."

Both males stopped, glaring at each other until they slowly backed away from one another. Kal shadow-jumped to my side instantly and wrapped his arm around my back, bringing my body closer to his in a protective gesture.

Uncle Cass's pale face took me in before he spoke, "I never thought I would find you, kiddo. I'm so happy to see you made it to your mother's realm. I'm sorry for the way you had to come here, but you are safe regardless."

I tried walking out of Kal's hold to go to Cassius, but his grip tightened on my waist, "I'm not safe, Uncle Cass. I fled from my grandmother's and my aunt's house early this morning. Whoever is after me found me there." I looked up at Kal, poking my finger into one of his solid pecs, "I was lucky this stalker was hanging around to save me from being attacked any further in the woods."

Kal looked down at me and sighed, "I have told you several times, Enayah, that I was only present to guard you."

"I know, but you have to see from my point of view that it looks pretty stalkerish." I rolled my eyes at him, which I did often with this exasperating male.

Uncle Cass cleared his throat, looking from Kal and then back to me, "Looks like you have been busy since you've been gone, Raine. I'm happy you finally found a male's attention."

"Oh–uh, no, I met Kal yesterday. I kicked his ass at a fighting competition." I paused, looking up at Kal with a smug smile across my face, but he wasn't paying attention to me, his eyes solely glued to Cassius. "Not too bad for a girl, though, huh?" I said, flourishing my hair behind my back, trying to lighten the mood.

"No, not bad at all." Cass chuckled. "I'm impressed; it's usually hard for females to beat the male shadow-jumpers unless they are one themselves. Is there something you aren't telling me?" Uncle Cass asked.

I frowned at him. He knew full well I hadn't come into those powers, "No, Uncle Cass. You know as well as I do that I never possessed that ability. Dad said it would have presented itself before I became a teenager, and it never has."

Kal spoke up just then. "I get you two are having a reunion, but," he turned to Cass with a frown etched on his face, "I need to know. Why were you snooping around in my home?"

I peered at the male I grew up with my entire life and frowned, as well. "How did you find me?"

He breathed heavily, stroking a hand through his hair before answering, "I suppose I need to get to the point of my visit. Firstly, I was 'snooping' to make sure you were indeed the male I was looking for. I presume you know the male Gezr?"

"Yes, he is the one who asked me to watch after Raine. After one of his friends advised him, I would be the one who needed to do it." Then, Kal's eyes lit up with realization, "Wait, you're the male who asked Gezr to convince me to help, aren't you?"

Uncle Cass inclined his head and answered, "I am. Gezr is an old friend. After one of my many visits to the Seer in Ozryn, I sought him out. The Seer saw you, Kalpheus. She told me you would be the one to keep Raine safe when trouble came calling. And you would be one to keep her safe through all of it." He paused briefly, "And I was in your home because Gezr told me the general area in which to find you. I was trying to determine if I had the correct one before moving on."

"That answers both our questions, I suppose. But, Uncle Cass," I breathed deeply, wondering if he knew what I was about to tell him. "You know Mom was killed, right? You have to understand that I can't go back to AshFiera. I have nothing back home, as both my mom and dad are gone. Here I have my Gigi and Aunt Samara. And that's only if I can stop whoever is hunting me. So I'm confused as to why you would be here?"

With unshed tears, I stared at him, longing to go and hug him, to let him embrace me with his arms, but Kal wasn't letting me go. He was so tense beside me that his grip was almost punishing, like he was waiting for Uncle Cass to do something to hurt me.

He straightened and reached behind him, pulling a box out to hold in front of him. Gripping onto it, he looked sorrowful. "Raine, it'll be crucial for you to listen to everything I tell you. I need you to believe that what your mother and I did was to protect you."

"What did you and Mom do, Uncle Cassius?" I whispered. My heart started pounding out of control, and a hum deafened my ears as the silence stretched between us. Was I ready for what was to come next? I didn't know, but I needed answers to questions he was beginning to draw forth.

"Your father is alive, Raine. He was never missing. And, unfortunately, he is the one who hired those Shadow Assassins. They were supposed to take you from your mom and deliver you to him. They were never supposed to hurt her." He said with anguish written across his face.

"What? How is that possible? My father is alive, and you're telling me he is the reason my mother is now dead?" Anger started bubbling up from inside—my body heating to an uncontrollable level, like I was a volcano about to erupt.

Uncle Cass shook his head, interrupting the growing rage that welled inside, "No–Raine. There's something else. Your mother isn't dead. She was barely alive when they had shadow-jumped, but your father healed her as soon as he had her. Now he holds her captive, waiting for you to come home."

The spell of anger broke immediately, and I sobbed, "What? M-my mother is alive?" Staring at Uncle Cass, he stepped forward. He still had the box in his hand, and he was fiddling with it now, drawing my attention.

"I have something for you. Your mother entrusted it to me. She took it from you a few days before the incident and gave it to me for safekeeping. I'm so sorry, Raine. We knew what was coming; we just didn't comprehend when, and she didn't want to risk you getting into his hands with your powers." He said, extending his arm to hand me the box he held.

I didn't touch it. And with hints of rolling rage beneath my breath, I uttered, "I don't understand. I never really had my powers. Mom told me she didn't know why they never came forth. Even with hints of it here and there. Was that a lie? What is the truth? Tell me, Cassius."

"I will tell you everything, Raine." He said, defeated and saddened by my hostility.

I listened while Kal stood beside me, his arm still holding me tight. I would need his strength and support. He was the best thing that had walked into my life at this point, and I had to keep myself level-headed when I found out what was to come next.

Cassius first told the story of why my father 'disappeared'.

"One of your father's close advisers visited your home one day. And your mother overheard them discussing the need to become more aggressive with your training. They wanted to push you further and bring in a witch, who wasn't Pandora, to force your powers to manifest early. Lazarus told the unknown male he was close to breaking through, and you were coming along beautifully with your strength, but your father was greedy and wanted more from you."

I was trying to take it all in. Was my father the villain in my life? The question swirled around in my head as Uncle Cass continued, "So, Pandora met with me and some of my close comrades to hatch a plan to lock your father up. She was trying to keep him away from you, only to protect you, I promise.

"We understood there was an important job your Father wouldn't pass up, so when he jumped into his safe house in the city of Ozryn, we had coordinated with several jumpers who were waiting for him. They injected him with a liquid that's too complex to explain and understand, but it would stop him from shadow-jumping out of the home. Once that took hold, a witch from the human realm helped in creating tungsten manacles. It seemed like a more permanent solution, so we shackled him with it and threw him into the cells that are below 'The Palace of Darkness' in the middle of Ozryn."

That answered a few questions, but more emerged to take their place.

"But how exactly did he escape Uncle Cass? And how long was he down there? And how did my mother hide my powers from not only him but from me as well?" I asked.

"Your Father had been in prison for the majority of the time. He was good at making friends with some of the most dangerous shadow-jumpers, who were also locked up below with him. They helped him escape his prison with outside help after only being captive for three years.

"Before we found out your Father escaped, Your Mother spelled the necklace your Father gave you. She did this right after his imprisonment. It was on one of the trips you both took to Martslocke and procured the binding spell from a witch living in Ozryn. This witch would travel to the village often to visit the shopkeeper of The Healing Shadows. So, Pandora spelled the necklace to hold and mute your growing powers. She understood it wouldn't be long before you finally manifested them one day."

Another question popped into my head. I needed Uncle Cass to answer, "If he escaped after only three years, why didn't he come for me then? Why now?"

Piercing his lips, he thought momentarily before answering, "I'm not sure, Raine. At first, your mother and I were just as confused. But we think he might have been gathering up his loyal shadow-jumpers to aid him, like your mother had done before we imprisoned him. He most likely did it when the time came to kidnap you from her."

"I still don't understand, though. What is so special about me that my father is going through all this to get to me? I'm just a girl with powers that were taken from her, who barely dares to defend herself. I am nobody and I'm nothing."

Kal turned my body towards him, gently grabbing my face with both hands and tilting my head so I would look up at him. His thumbs rubbed back and forth along my cheekbones as he spoke, "Don't speak of yourself like that. You may not know me very well, but I intend to change that. And understand me now when I say this, I speak the truth. You are something else, my Enayah. I feel it deep inside myself whenever I look at you. There is a power hidden deep beneath that is aching to be released. I will be with you every step of the way to figure out how to bring it to the surface. You will overcome the fear that dug its claws so profoundly into you."

Uncle Cass walked up, still holding the box, and said, "Your mother wanted me to ensure you had this back when it was time. She wanted me to clarify that she doesn't want you to come for her. If your father gets hold of you, she doesn't know what he would do with you." He placed the box in my hand and stepped back. "We are trying to figure out how to rescue your mom, though. It might take some time. So please, Raine, promise me that whatever happens next, you will not go to AshFiera."

Clutching the box, I shook my head, "I can't promise you that, and you know it. She's my mom, Cass. She sacrificed herself so I would have a head start fleeing our home. I need to try to help release her from my Father's hold." I took a deep breath to control the shaking that started, "I need to try at least. She never once portrayed my father as a villain. I don't know if he truly is, but I'm willing to risk it to bring her to safety."

Looking up at Kal, I smiled at him. Stepping back out of his hold, I looked at the box Uncle Cass gave me. It was black with matte flames adorning all around. My mother must have replaced the old, tattered box I had with it, as this was new; I had never seen it before.

I slid the top off, and inside lay my flamed Ashix locket. It was wrapped in the same black fabric my father had initially used when he gifted it to me.

Grabbing hold of the jewelry, my hand involuntarily locked and closed over it. I couldn't release the locket, and the box fell to my feet, forgotten.

A sensation slowly trickled out of the locket into my hand, as it crawled up my arm; a hum intensified beneath the surface. Suddenly, I was on my knees, one hand on the ground below me while the other still clutched the locket. I brought my hand to my chest, close to my heart. A horrendous scream escaped as purple, electrically charged lights shot out and dove into my open mouth, and a humming buzz took over my entire body.

The light dissipated, and my body fell onto the grass. I curled up on my side, cocooning myself from the lingering shocks. Faintly, I heard Kal yelling at Uncle Cass, but I couldn't make out what was being said. Everything was muffled, as if my head was being submerged underwater.

A few more minutes passed, and I was finally able to start swimming out of the depths of the haze that came over me. Then I heard it: grunting and growling, along with the thuds of someone being struck.

Uncle Cass and Kal were further away from me, and I studied them as they were back to fighting each other.

I rolled my eyes and thought, *fucking males and their egos. Now, what were they squabbling about?*

I sat up, staring at them lazily, my gaze on Kal. He was a glorious fighter, graceful in his moves. His instinct told him where to strike and when. Admiring the globes of his backside, I was interrupted when they turned, and I caught a glimpse of Uncle Cass's hand locked onto Kal's throat, gripping tightly. Kal held onto Cassius' arm, attempting to break free. And then, Uncle Cass's other arm pulled back in slow motion. Aiming right for Kal's heart with his fingers spread, readying to rip it out in a single move.

"No!" I shouted. Lifting myself off the ground with lightning speed, but I wasn't going to make it fast enough to knock his arm out of the way of Kal's heart. So, I raised my hand, letting the electricity flow from my fingers, tendrils escaping the appendages like liquid flowing down a waterfall's edge. The purple bolts shot out, clamping onto Cass's hand, stopping it from going further.

Both males were motionless in mere seconds, their heads turning in unison to look at me in shock.

I was breathless from running, and now, holding onto Uncle Cass' hand, it was taking quite the effort to keep him still.

Quirking an eyebrow, I asked them both, "Well? Are you going to let each other go, or will I have to separate you two idiots with a jolt?"

Looking back at one another, they nodded and let go. Still holding Uncle Cass's hand, I decided to test my power and willed his hand to slap him in the face. With his free hand, he was trying to hold it back, making me giggle for once in days.

"Alright, alright, I give. Raine! Let—Ow!—Go of my hand." Uncle Cass said with annoyance.

"Say 'uncle'," I grinned more wildly at him.

He glared, like I was a petulant child, and maybe I was, but this newfound power I suddenly had was intoxicating, "Seriously? Are we reverting to being childish, Raine?"

I decided to continue, looking at him, patiently waiting.

"UNCLE, alright, uncle!" He finally relented, making me smirk even more.

Kal was standing a few feet away from Cassius, watching our exchange. His arms crossed, and his legs spread apart, eyes glittering with want and a hint of proudness.

Goddess, he was so handsome, especially the way he was at that moment. I wanted to get to know him better. An intense connection flowed between us. It was even stronger now that I had my powers reclaimed and unmuted. The unmistakable pull of our souls entwined within each other.

This was something I would explore more with him when we were alone and didn't have company lingering around.

I looked back at Uncle Cass, "That will teach you not to mess—"

My words cut off abruptly when I heard Kal's howl. When I looked back at him, a smaller male stood in front of him, holding a dripping dagger that had left his body. Memories flashed back to when my mother was stabbed before I fled, and something snapped inside.

Hot anger bubbled up from the pits of my stomach, and I unleashed my lightning. Grabbing hold of the male by the throat with those sparkling purple tendrils. I dangled him off the ground and slowly approached with a sneer.

Looking at his face, I gasped, "You—I remember you. You were trying to walk my mother and me home. It was the day before I had to flee the property and my dying mother."

He didn't say a word; his gaze assessed my powers with wide eyes as he tried to glance down at what held his neck.

Glowering at the thin, pale male, my words flowed to him laced with venom, "You work for my father, don't you?" I asked, but didn't wait for his response, "You sought us out to walk my mother and me home, and then what? Lure us into my father's clutches!? If I had known then what I do now, I would have sunk my dagger into your throat myself. Instead, you get the first taste of my powers, the current running through my veins just before your death."

Without hesitation, I quickly pushed the jolting through and dropped the male. He didn't move or breathe, and I left him where his unmoving body remained.

Looking over to Kal, I could see he was still standing. His hand clutched to his abdomen, and where the blood was pouring out moments before, it slowed its flow.

I ran to him, ghosting my hands over his, "Kal, Goddess. I don't know what happened just now. I—I snapped, seeing that dagger dripping with blood. It reminded me of when I thought my mother had been killed. I should have come to you first." My heart was pounding, and guilt swept into my soul. I could have lost him before I even had him.

With his other hand that wasn't covered in blood, he slid it to the back of my neck and gripped the hair at the base of my head, holding me still while he put his forehead to mine. "My Enayah, never doubt for a moment how proud you've made me. Look at you. You stood up for yourself and me. You are a vision."

"But, you're hurt. We need to bring you inside, and that wound will need stitches, I'm sure."

Uncle Cass stepped in with the dagger the sickly male brought with him, in his hands, "Kal, the dagger—I'm afraid it was dipped in the concoction we used on Raine's Father. You won't be able to shadow-jump for a while. And healing might take a little longer." He looked at me with determination in his eyes and sorrow, "I don't want you to return to AshFiera, Raine. Under no circumstances should you go home—no matter the means. Let us help rescue your mother and bring her back here. Then, once you're both together, we'll find a place to hide you. He has the same magic paralyzing drug we once made. It was only a matter of time before he had it himself. We'll need to be more vigilant now."

I looked at him, shocked that he would ask me such a thing, and everything just confirmed I needed to get back to AshFiera that much sooner. He knew my mother meant everything, who knew what my father would do to her, "I can't promise that, Uncle Cass. I have to try. You can shadow-jump us to a nearby hideout in AshFiera, and we can come up with a plan-"

He interrupted me with a finality that sank into the pits of my stomach, "No, I can not jump with you. I need to leave and make extra preparations with the others. They need to know what your Father now possesses. Please forgive me, little Ashix. I can not go back on my word with your mother. I need to protect you from him. It's my duty and vow."

Then he left. Up and shadow-jumped without even saying goodbye. Like my Father had done, Uncle Cass even used the nickname my father gave me to push the point. I knew he was doing it for my own good, not bringing me to where I was needed. And I didn't like it.

I wasn't going to let it slow me down, though. Only one thing would prolong the inevitable, and that was ensuring Kal was healing. From what I gathered, it would be a few days of recovery before Kal could jump with me. I would take care of him and, in the meantime, convince him to help me. I eyed Kal, walking up to help him in the house so I could care for him.

Kal held up his hand, seeing the look on my face, "Yes, I will take you to AshFiera. But not yet. I need time to heal, and you heard your Uncle. It will be a few days before I can even jump. I'm all for kicking some ass. Especially to a male who disavows his own family."

"Thank you, Kal. You have no idea how much that means to me. Now, let's get inside and clean you up."

We entered his home, and I first noticed a large, sparkling, clean fireplace that looked as if it had never been used. On the ground in front of the nook was a giant sheep-skin rug that looked cozy.

What I wouldn't give to sit in front of a fire on a snowy night. With a hot cup of cocoa, naked next to Kal after having sex on said rug.

Okay, you fucking perv, one thing at a time! You haven't even done the deed before!

I daydreamed about those activities, not noticing Kal sneak up behind me. He was holding a first aid kit and a towel.

"Here, let me grab those. Go sit on the couch and take your shirt off." I instructed him.

He obeyed my command without complaint. And I followed him over to the couch, kneeling before him. He opened his legs and widened them to allow me to scoot closer in between. Grabbing a pillow beside him on the sofa, I placed it on the floor to allow myself more comfort on the hard surface. Placing my hand on his thigh while reaching over for the kit, I gripped him and was greeted by sculpted marble under my fingers. His body tensed, and the muscle in his thigh jumped from the contact. Looking up at him before I began my ministrations, his face was a mask of serious masculinity. He didn't give anything away, but I knew my touch affected him.

Grabbing the first aid again and a wet towel, I began to wash away the blood that had dried around the edges of the dagger wound. Blood slowly trickled out of the opening to the edge of his pants. My gaze momentarily drawn to the trail of dark hair disappearing beneath, I continued.

With him cleaned up, I began to stitch his skin back together. My hands were steady, but my eyes wandered over his rock-hard abs again and toned chest where his tattoo of the stars was visible. I wanted to put my tongue all over him. The urge to do so grew, and I leaned closer to him, licking my lips.

Kal cleared his throat, and my eyes shot up to his face. He was grinning widely, letting his fangs show, and then he bit his bottom lip. A soft moan escaped my throat, and I looked back down to focus on what I was doing.

Why was that so hot? Did I want his fangs to nibble on my body?

Sexual tension filled the room. The urge to finish and step away from him was like a sharp prick of awareness.

I finished stitching him up quickly and started picking up the remnants of the first aid kit. Before I got off my knees, Kal grabbed my upper arm gently, stopping me, and leaned his body forward. His other hand glided over my jaw and held me. "Thank you." He said, his eyes shining brightly in the morning sunlight.

It was the only thing he said before his lips were a breath away from mine. He stopped before they touched, waiting to see if I would pull back—silent permission. When I didn't move away, he gently pressed his lips into mine. Closing my eyes, I savored the pressure we created. I barely believed what we were doing. It was my first kiss, and I had no idea how to execute it correctly or if it was pleasurable for him.

Then, panic started settling in.

As if he sensed my thoughts, the tip of his warm tongue

tenderly poked the seam of my lips. I opened my mouth and let him in, his tongue dancing along with mine. It was breathtaking, like nothing I had ever experienced in my life.

As our tongues continued their delicate assault against one another, a tug began deep in my center. I shifted my legs to soothe the ache, but it wasn't enough. Leaning into his body, a pained groan left his throat. Our kissing stopped abruptly, and I realized we had gotten carried away, and I had possibly hurt him.

"Kal, oh no. I'm so sorry, I think we need to–uh–take a break. Did I hurt you?" My voice laced with concern as I examined the wound I had patched up.

"I'm good, Raine. Just a little sore." His smile was like a flower blooming first thing in the morning—*beautiful*. My heart skipped, and I grinned like a fool at him.

"Gods, Raine, you are so fucking beautiful when you smile at me like that. I never want to see anything else grace your face but that."

I nodded, my stomach growling for the second time that day, interrupting our moment. I snickered, shaking my head. "I should eat something. It will never give up, no matter how much I ignore it."

"Alright, my Enayah. Let's fill that demanding body of yours." He said, his eyes darkening for a split second before returning to a grin, but that lingering stare of want never left him as we moved apart.

Chapter Eleven
Raine

While I put away the first aid kit in the bathroom, Kal was in the kitchen preparing something for us to eat. I thought the day drug along, but when I glanced at the clock hanging on the wall, it read past midday.

I decided to make my way into the kitchen, which was located off the living room, behind the couch. Walking through an archway, it was warmly lit with rustic tones that were inviting and homey. Mahogany cabinets lined both sides of the room. The countertops were made of a dark, smoky stone that held several utensils and a bowl of ripe apples.

Ogling those apples, I licked my lips and reached for one. But Kal was already prepared and held one in his hands. I smiled at him as he gave it to me.

"Eat this while I make us a few sandwiches."

Inclining my head, I walked around the island and sat on one of the stools facing him. Biting into the apple, my mouth full, I was curious about Kal, "Tell me about yourself, Kal. I'm interested in how you grew up in AshFiera."

"There isn't much to tell Raine. I didn't have a great upbringing."

I stopped mid-bite of my apple, staring questioningly at him, "I would very much like to know, though."

I shrugged when he quirked an eyebrow, "I wasn't able to talk to many people while living there. Mom and I would visit the village near our home once a week. And when I did attempt to speak to anyone, especially the males, no one gave me the time of day. I don't know if it was because of who my mother was or if my father was the one who inspired that fear. But it was often lonely, and I didn't know if anyone had an interest or a life that was similar to mine since they all ignored me."

"I doubt anyone's life or interests were similar to yours by any measure." He said. Like being the daughter of a witch and a Shadow Assassin was an immense accomplishment that not many others could or would achieve.

He finished making the sandwiches and handed one to me. It was a regular old PBJ. I took a bite and moaned at the creamy, rich, nutty flavor of the peanut butter, perfectly mixed with the slightly gritty and sweet tartness of the raspberry jam. I looked up as I was about to take another bite and caught Kal watching my mouth with his opened somewhat. I snickered and returned to eating the delicious morsel while waving my hand for him to continue.

"As I said, I didn't have the best upbringing. Both of my parents were Shadow Assassins. They usually went out on jobs together, and they were inseparable, often joking and laughing, and crazy in love with each other. They cared more about themselves than me, their only child. One day, they left on an assignment and never returned. I was young, maybe five or six at the time. One of my parents' closest friends was watching me while they were out, and they got news of their passing. They kept me for a short time until, at the age of ten, I did my first shadow-jump. I was the youngest shadow-jumper ever to be recorded. The youngest before me was fourteen."

He paused and took a deep breath, almost like he relived a painful memory.

"I was sent off to a recruitment facility where I trained extensively until I was sixteen. That's when they finally let me have my first job. And it's been that way ever since."

"Wow, I'm sorry you had to go through all that. It doesn't seem fair for you not to have a somewhat normal childhood. Considering who your parents were, of course. It hurts my heart to know they cared very little for you, too." I wanted to wrap him up in my arms and never let go. My soul was yearning to soothe his.

"What was your childhood like?" He inquired, obviously ready for a change of conversation.

"Hard–but not as tough as yours. My father was demanding, making me train with him every day. Sometimes, we would go hunting, but those always became lessons in themselves. My only reprieve was my mother as a buffer and Beauty." Thinking of the Ashix, I wondered how she was faring without seeing me at home. Did she miss me? Or did she move on, thinking I abandoned her?

"Who is Beauty?" Kal asked, distracting me from my other inner questions.

"She's my companion, an Ashix that my mother said had been a gift from the Goddess herself. The beast claimed me as her own. She sometimes sat on a boulder near my home and watched Father and me. When he noticed her perched there, he always went easier on me. I think he was secretly terrified of her, which is why I loved it when she was there. It gave me a break from his grueling brutality on most days. Then, after my father left, she started coming around almost daily. It was rare for her to be gone for long."

"The day your home was attacked, I never saw her. I didn't detect any Ashix around the falls or woods either." Kal mentioned, causing me to pause and look at him.

"Huh, now that you mention it, I didn't either when I ran that morning. Odd. I wonder if the beasts sensed what was going to happen." I hesitated, "But that doesn't make sense because Beauty would have been around regardless. She always knew when something negative was in the air and would always be in sight of our home."

I needed to go back home soon, not only to save my mother but also to find out what happened to Beauty when all of this was over. I trusted she was safe, but I couldn't be sure. Something deep down inside was nagging at the subconscious part of my mind, but I couldn't let it get in the way for now.

We finished our sandwiches and left the kitchen to return to the living room. The box with my locket was on the table in front of the couch. I longed to put it on, but worried it would mute my newly acquired powers again.

Kal caught me staring at it, "I believe the spell your mother put on it no longer exists. Not since it gave you back your powers when you touched it again."

It was logical and made sense, but I hesitated for a moment.

Taking a chance, I snatched it out of the box. Exhaling when nothing happened, and still sensed the surge running through me.

Rubbing my thumb over the texture of the locket, I smiled. My mother was clever, hiding my powers in this small keepsake I rarely took off my neck. Out of habit, I opened the clasp, and a tightly folded piece of paper fell onto the floor.

Kal leaned down and picked it up. He handed it over to me. Our fingers grazed each other, the electricity intensifying, leaving me panting. But then he pulled back, and the link was silent again.

My attention was drawn back to the paper. I slowly unfolded it, careful not to rip any parts of the thin material. Once opened, I swallowed down a lump forming and looked at Kal. "It's a note from my mom."

My dearest Raine,

I'm so sorry for what I have put you through. I hope you will forgive me one day for what I had to do to your powers. I only wanted to protect you, and I would pay any cost necessary. Even if it meant I lost your trust in the process. Know that no matter what, I love you with all my heart. And if Cassius finds you and he tells you everything we have kept from you, promise me you will stay away from AshFiera. If I am still alive, I can take care of myself. Please, Raine, I know what you are thinking. I can't have you risking your life or freedom for mine. I'm not sure what your father would do if he ever got hold of you, and it scares me. I would like to imagine he wouldn't do anything sinister, but he is not the male I fell in love with all those years ago.

I love you, my little Ashix, and I hope you live a long, beautiful life and never look back.

With all the love my soul pours into yours,
Mom

A small wet spot formed on the letter, and I realized that tears were coming from me. I was angry at her for not telling me the whole truth about my powers and keeping my father's disappearance a secret. But I knew I would forgive her. I could never be truly mad at her because I understood her reasoning, even if it was extreme.

Staring at the letter, rereading it, a deep-rooted unease started as if I was missing something. Then I noticed a blank section that looked like something had been written but then smudged—not wholly erased but unintelligible for anyone to read correctly.

It was frustrating trying to decipher if this was a hidden message.

How in the hell was I supposed to unscramble it if it was?

Sitting on the couch staring at the paper, my thoughts turned dark. My father was a monster. Did he ever truly love my mother, or me, for that matter? The rage I hid was rearing its ugly head again. But instead of feeling like my blood was boiling, it was circulating, buzzing, and crackling. A breeze in the room was picking up faster and faster. Whipping anything light around in a circle like I was in the middle of a tornado. It was getting stronger and out of control. A crash sounded beside me as something broke from the force of the wind that seemed to be coming from me, cascading faster the more my emotions spiraled out of control.

The next thing I knew, a pair of hands grabbed my face. A muffled, deep, rich, sultry voice was calling my name. Those hands moved from my face to my waist, lifting my body and placing me onto a lap.

I shook my head, trying to clear it of the hateful haze. One hand left my waist to hold onto my face again, and I finally remembered that I was sitting next to Kal. Except now I was sitting on him. His eyebrows were drawn with worry. I sighed as the wind died down, bringing calmness once more. The graze of his fingers was magical, almost like the way Gigi and Aunt Samara could calm me down with a single touch.

He felt good. I had never straddled a man before in this way. It was different in the ring, as that was about showcasing your ability to overpower your opponent. In this position, it was something else entirely.

Leaning forward, being careful of the wound on his stomach, I kissed him.

It started as soft and tender. Molding into something heady and uncontrollable, I gripped what little I could of Kal's hair. Pushing my tongue into his mouth while he let out a growl, causing goosebumps to form on my arms and little shivers to run down my body.

Gripping my ass with both hands, he squeezed. The movement caused the center of my body to line up over his hard cock just right. I released a moan when the perfect pressure was on my clit. As I began to rock slowly over him, our breaths mingled with one another, and the tension built between us. Kal gripped the back of my hair in one hand and pulled, exposing my neck to him. He kissed below my ear, moving down slowly, nibbling as he went. When he reached the hollow of my neck and shoulder, he bit harder. I let out a gasp as my rocking became jerky and uneven.

"Goddess, Kal–Yes!"

"Mmm, come for me, my Enayah. Let me see you shatter."

His words were a chisel breaking through glass. My body did as he commanded, and I fell into the sweet abyss of pleasure. Kal followed shortly after with a release of his own, his deep moan vibrating against my breasts. The wetness of his cum was evident, spotting his pants from the passion we shared.

The pleasure I had experienced was euphoric and

flowed throughout my body, leaving my limbs pliant. Never had I experienced anything so sinfully blissful.

"Kal, I need to tell you something. I have never been with anyone before. What we did was a first for me." I stammered.

His eyes focused on mine. And as he gazed at me without a single expression crossing his face, I fidgeted in his lap. Feeling like an idiot, I started to get up as I realized I was confessing to him that I had never been with anyone else before. But he gripped my thighs, rubbing his thumbs on the inner skin as my nightgown had ridden up.

"Raine, it's okay to be inexperienced. There's nothing wrong with it. It makes me want you even more. Knowing I will be the only male to have touched you and to have the honor of listening to your cries of pleasure. We will take it slow, and I will show you everything you missed." He grinned widely, showing off a dimple I hadn't noticed until I was close to him.

Relief flooded my languid body. I murmured, "Thank you. I worried you would look at me differently."

"Now, that is absurd. I would never look at you differently. Even before you met me, I watched over you. Witnessing you grieve was the hardest thing to glimpse when I couldn't be there to hold you and soothe your heart. But then, I enjoyed watching you flourish in this world. It was dazzling, and I knew I needed you in my life. For me, this is so much more than guarding you, my Enayah."

His confession sent butterflies flipping in my stomach. After being ignored by others for so long, I never thought a male would be interested in me. It was intoxicating. To be wanted by someone and cared for. I had to admit, at first, he frightened me, but slowly over the last few hours, he nestled his way into my heart. It seemed so sudden, but something was screaming at me to trust it and keep going.

My attention was drawn back to the letter my mother had left me.

"I should probably get up from your lap. Something is off with the letter from my mother, almost as if a part of it is missing, erased, or smudged." Getting up from Kal's lap, I sat beside him on the couch and reached for the locket.

"I'm just going to head to the bathroom, clean myself, and change while you look that over." He said, while the cushion of his couch bounced as he got up.

"Okay, I'll be right here."

Kal walked over to his bedroom and shut the door. A moment later, sounds of running water emitted from what I believed was an attached bathroom in his room.

With the locket in my hand, I opened it and brought forth the letter. Unquestionably, there was a missing piece on the paper. Did my mother intend for this to be left blank? Or was I meant to uncover what was hidden beneath?

Placing the letter on the table in front of me, I held a hand above and let out tiny zaps of lightning, willing the page to reveal the missing words if they even existed. When nothing happened, I used both hands.

Still, nothing happened.

Getting off the couch in frustration, I paced back and forth while my mind reeled on what I could try next.

I was about to grab the page and rip it to shreds in my frustration when words started appearing. Holding my breath, I waited for it to finish before I picked it up and read what my mother meant for only me to find.

Raine, if you have figured out how to uncover this, I have one request. We have an ancestral spell book that I used to open the portal to AshFiera. You need to find that book and close all the portals I created in that event. It will keep you safe and prevent the shadow-jumpers from entering Earth. I understand I am asking a lot, but I am confident this is the only way to keep him from reaching you.

Why didn't I think about my family's spell-book to get back to AshFiera in the first place? To hell with closing the portals, though. I was going to rescue my mom. We didn't have to wait for Kal to recover his ability to shadow-jump. Who knew how long that would take anyway?

It might take a few days to recover the spell book, which was perfect. It gave Kal's wound enough time to heal, mostly. But I had to get back to Gigi's and find my phone to call her and Aunt Sam. Like an idiot, I didn't have their numbers memorized.

There was no telling if they had the book in the house or if they had hidden it elsewhere. Only they knew where it currently was. I just hoped Kal would walk with me back to the house to retrieve it.

Speaking of Kal, he strolled out from the bedroom in only shorts, his hair and chest still glistening from his shower. He was even more sexy while dripping wet. Gulping, I cleared my throat. "Hey, I–uh, uncovered a secret message my mother left." My eyes trailed along his chest, down to where the lines of his hips peeked out. I swallowed, my throat dry as sand, before showing him the letter. "Here, read this, and then I have something to ask you."

He quickly took the paper and read the letter. Looking up at me, he grinned, "This is brilliant. We need to find that book and find out what is inside that would help you." He placed the letter back down on the table, turning his full attention on me. "Now, you have something to ask?"

"Yeah, I need you to come back to my house with me so I can grab my phone."

"No. Absolutely not, Raine. I won't risk bringing you back there when they could have someone camped out in the house or even around the property." He interrupted, which only grated on my nerves as we were this close to helping my mom.

"I don't care, Kal. I need my phone to call my Gigi and Aunt. I don't have their numbers memorized. It was easy to press a simple button, as it was already programmed into the phone. How else are we supposed to figure out where the book is?" Standing from the couch away from his intoxicating manly musk, I crossed my arms over one another and tapped my foot on the floor, waiting for his answer.

Looking me up and down, he scoffed, "Fine–but! You will listen to every command I give you, and if I tell you to run, you fucking run. Got it? I won't lose you when I can't follow you back to AshFiera yet."

Nodding and sauntering up to him, I wrapped my arms around his neck. Peering into his eyes, I leaned forward, placing tiny kisses on his lower lip and whispering, "Thank you."

It was still early enough in the day for the sun to be out and shining brightly. He got dressed in his leathers, and I changed out of my nightgown and into one of his sweats and shirts. They were huge on me, so I had to tie knots to keep them from sliding off my body. When we got back to the house, I would grab some of my clothes. Not that I didn't enjoy wearing his, but I needed something that was mine.

Kal made a point of looking at an old-school map to find our locations. I discovered my Gigi's house and determined it was only a few hours' walk.

Then, we set off into the woods toward my home, where there was a possibility we might run into more trouble along the way.

Chapter Twelve
Raine

T he walk to the house was excruciatingly long. But we made it before the sun dipped below the horizon. Kal was ever observant, scanning the trees and stopping me abruptly when he heard a twig snap. It turned out it was a deer foraging for food near us.

"It's just a deer, Kal. I'm pretty sure it's not going to turn into an assassin and strangle us." I huffed out a laugh, rolling my eyes. "So dramatic, I don't hear anyone walking or scrounging around in the house. I think the coast is clear, captain."

"Very funny, Enayah. That tongue of yours will get you into trouble someday. But you are right; I don't hear anyone either. Let's go through the window anyway, just to be sure."

"Not like I haven't heard that one before," I said.

"Heard what before my little star?" Kal asked.

"That what comes out of my mouth will get me into trouble one day," I said, smiling.

We ran across the yard and up to my window. Kal gripped my waist with both hands, hoisting me, and then ever so gently pushed my ass further up and inwards. I wasn't quite so graceful as I fell onto the floor.

"You good there, Raine?" Kal called from below the window.

"Yeah, all good, just clumsy and not nimble like a pussy cat would be."

Moving into the room, I started to walk around my bed as Kal climbed in shortly after. Viewing the splintered door and the tossed bedroom, I frantically searched the floor near my bedside table. Some clothes had been ripped from my closet and half haphazardly thrown onto the floor, which is where I found my phone tucked under the pile.

Ugh, this is going to take forever to locate some decent clothes. Why did they tear them out of the closet and throw them all over?

"Do you have your phone? We need to leave soon and head back to my place fast." Kal's voice was edged with concern and worry. He was holding a hand to his injured stomach.

"Crap, did you rip your stitches open coming through the window?" I asked, worried that he did.

"No, I don't think so, but it doesn't feel good after leaping through."

"Let's go to the kitchen, then. Aunt Sam left her truck keys, and we can take it back to your place so we don't have to walk through the dark—especially if you hurt yourself. Plus, it will be faster."

He grabbed my arm, gazing out the window and then over to the hallway with nostrils flaring. "It needs to be quick; I don't have a good feeling if we stay here much longer."

Grabbing a couple of stretchy yoga pants and some

tanks, I picked them up from the floor, throwing them into a backpack I had stashed in the back of my closet.

After shoving the clothes inside, I walked through the hall and toward the kitchen. Stopping as I reached the living room, I winced when I saw the state of the remainder of the house.

"Goddess, they didn't leave anything untouched, did they? Fucking animals." I spat, knowing I would need to clean this up before Gigi came home. She ensured that everything was placed in its designated spot. It would blow her gasket, and she would fillet someone alive for how things were left.

The kitchen, as I walked through, was surprisingly untouched; I immediately spotted the keys hanging on the side of the cabinet closest to the patio door. I turned to Kal, jingling them at him.

"Forewarning, I never learned how to drive, but I have watched enough of Aunt Sam that I have the gist of the mechanics."

The keys were immediately snatched from my fingers, "Hey! I'm not going to kill us. I know not to drive like a maniac!"

"Don't care. I have driven human vehicles before, and I know I will be a better driver than you, someone with no experience."

Scoffing at him, I walked out the patio door, swaying my hips and not bothering to lock the door behind us as the handle was dangling down. An almost inaudible growl sounded behind me as Kal followed closely. Smiling to myself, I knew what I was doing with my hips. I wanted to elicit a reaction from him, and it made me giddy to know I was successful. The little jolt of power I held over a man was invigorating after years of not having this.

Kal was at the passenger truck door before me, and like a gentleman or gentlemale, he opened it, ushering me inside quickly—*pushy pants.*

Running around hurriedly to the other side of the truck, he sat down, and the truck slightly dipped on his side. Eyeing him, I turned to face the other way, covering my mouth with the back of my hand and giggling. Aunt Sam had the seat so far up to the steering wheel that it was comical to catch sight of him scrunched up and trying to adjust it back.

"Tight fit for you, Kal?"

Slowly, he moved his gaze in my direction and gave me a cocky smirk, "That's not the only tight fit I will be put into soon, my Enayah."

My cheeks heated, and I dissolved into laughter, "You know, for being in this precarious situation, it feels good to laugh and smile with someone again. I hope we can continue this way."

Shyness crept into my words. Having known Kal only briefly, it was apparent I was falling for the male. Was it too soon? Probably, but it felt so right, and deep down, something inside my body was saying, 'Yes—yes—yes!'

"We will, don't you worry. Your mom will be safe soon, and we can come back to the human world and close the portals. That's only if we haven't figured out how to deal with your father beforehand." He smiled, put the truck in drive, and headed back to his home.

The drive was shorter than the long walk we had endured earlier that day. It was late, and I didn't know if Gigi or Samara had their phones on.

I tried anyway, pacing in Kal's living room. On the second ring, Aunt Sam answered.

"Raine, girly, what a surprise! Normally, we have to call

you first. We just arrived at one of the ports about ten minutes ago. Perfect timing!"

"Hey, Aunt Sam, are you guys having a great time? I bet the weather is nice?"

"Oh, you have no idea. Every day, I am out by the pool catching those rays. Getting a nice tan going."

It was nice to hear that she had no worries. I would have to burst that and try not to worry Gigi or her any more than I had to. But they needed to understand what they could potentially walk into. Alternatively, they could make arrangements with Gage when they return; that was the best option for now.

"So, I need to speak with both you and Gigi. Is she around?" I asked, worried about how they would respond.

"Yeah, kiddo. She's right next to me. Want me to put it on speaker?"

Clearing my throat, I wasn't sure where they were on the ship, but I hoped they would judge if they needed to move.

"Yeah, only if it's safe from prying ears." I paused, listening to the sudden scraping on the other end. It sounded like she put the phone in her clothes and was now walking somewhere.

"Okay, we are both here." Aunt Sam said, followed by Gigi.

"Raine baby, I'm here too."

"Hi, Gigi. So–um, I have to tell you how sorry I am about your house first of all." Rip that band-aid off, since she might very well see it before I could fully get it back together.

"What do you mean? What happened to the house? Oh my goddess, Raine, are you hurt?" Panic and concern laced in Gigi's voice.

"I'm okay, Gigi. But the house is a bit messy inside. The Shadow Assassins who tried taking me back in AshFiera came after me there. But there is another thing that you should know first. Mom's best friend, Cassius, found me at my friend Kal's home and told me Mom wasn't dead. She's alive, and so is my father. That's not even the messed-up portion; he's the one who sent the assassins to bring me to him."

Silence descended on the other end, and I had to look at my phone to make sure I didn't lose the connection. "Hello? Are you guys still there?"

"Yes—Ahem. Sorry, that's a bit too much to take in all at once. I think your Gigi is still trying to process what you told us."

"I know it's a lot, but the male who is helping keep me safe is from AshFiera, and he was badly hurt. He can't jump with me for who knows how long. And mom left me a note mentioning the portal spell in our family's ancestral book. She said you guys would know where it's located."

Gigi cleared her throat, "We do know where it is. It's not in the house, though; it was entrusted to friends for safe-keeping. I didn't want your aunt to find the spell your mother used and go after her, so I had them take it. It's been in their care ever since she disappeared."

I glanced at Kal, who intently watched every fidget and movement I made, and nodded at him.

"That's great, I need it. In the note, Mom said the book contained a counter spell for the portals on Earth that could be used to close them. It would no longer allow anyone from AshFiera to shadow-jump here. Can—can you contact them?"

There was more silence on the other end, and then I

faintly heard whispering, as I was sure they were discussing whether to do it or not.

"I will do my best to get a hold of someone. It's late, and I am unsure if anyone will be awake at this hour," Gigi explained. I understood the time difference and knew it was near midnight here.

"Okay, let me know as soon as you find something out. Oh, before I forget. I have your truck, Aunt Sam. Kal knows how to drive human vehicles, so we took it to make traveling easier."

"Best not wreck my beautiful girl! I am trusting you with all her rusty glory." Aunt Samara scolded me playfully and dramatically.

Hanging up quickly, I ran a hand through my hair, snagging it in a curl, and collapsed onto the couch. Kal came around to sit next to me, lifting my feet into his lap. He started to rub at the soles, eliciting a long moan from me. Closing my eyes, we were able to sit here and be still. That stillness let my body drift off into a light sleep.

I was startled awake when my phone started ringing. Looking at the time, it was past two in the morning, and Aunt Samara's name popped up on my screen a second time.

"Hey, Aunt Sam. Sorry, we fell asleep on the couch." I said, looking over at Kal, asleep with my feet still held in his hands.

"Good news, kiddo. Gigi's friends, the Hacketts, are willing to meet with you tomorrow afternoon. I'll text you the details of their home address so you can map it. It's about a two-hour drive from our home."

"That's amazing news; thank you so much." I hesitated briefly. "I need you both to stay with Gage when you come back home. I know you are still away for a few more weeks.

But I'm unsure how long it will take to get Mom back and deal with Dad. It would kill me if anything happened to either one of you because of me."

"Don't worry. I have already talked to Gage. He is letting us crash with him until we know more. He's worried about you but knows you are more than capable of handling yourself. I mentioned another man was with you, and he went into big brother mode. But then he calmed down when I mentioned Kal's name. I can't wait to meet him, Raine. Gage had nothing but great things to say about him, and if he is keeping my niece safe, then that's good enough for me."

"Heh, I can't wait for you guys to meet him, too. It's late here, and Kal is sleeping next to me." Whispering, I glanced back at him again, and his eyes were open, lazily gazing at me.

"Alright, babes, talk to you soon, keep in touch. We love you." She demanded.

Dropping the phone onto the table, my gaze found Kal's again, "Did you hear everything?"

"Mostly yes, I'm glad they got in touch with their friends."

"Me too. We need to get some sleep, though. It sounds like it's a bit of a drive, and we should leave early to be safe." Pulling my feet from his hands, I stood. "Where can I sleep?"

Kal was on his feet and encased my body within his arms, "You can sleep in the bed with me. I promise to be on my best behavior tonight."

Smiling at Kal, cheeks heating up once more, I said. "Alright, I suppose I'll sleep in your bed. I'm sure it'll be more comfortable than the couch anyway."

With one arm still slung around my back, the other one

scooped up my thighs. Kal held me tightly to his body while making his way to the bedroom.

Depositing me on one side, he walked to the other and stripped his shirt. It gave me a small tease of his rolling muscles before he slid under the covers.

Climbing under the blankets right after him, I faced away on my side. He tugged my body into his and draped an arm over my stomach. It didn't take long, and I was blissfully pulled into darkness within the comfort of his arms.

Chapter Thirteen
Kal

Raine was a bundle of nerves as we headed to her family friend's home. They had been keeping the ancestral book safe all these years. And are willing to meet with Raine and me after her grandmother spoke with someone.

It was only a two-hour drive, but Raine was frantically bouncing her right leg up and down most of the way. Several times, I had to reach over and place my hand on her thigh to get her to look over at me. When she did, the nervous habit usually died down for a few minutes, and then she was back to bouncing.

"Raine, everything will be fine. They will give you back the book, and then we can be on our way." Trying to reassure her, but she shook her head, looking out the truck's window, and watching the trees blur past.

"But what if they don't? What if they want something from me? I don't have anything to give, and it's mine, right? The book, I mean, they have to give it back. Gigi trusted them enough with it. She trusts them to give it back, so they will. They have to. I don't know how long we have left before my father becomes impatient and does something disastrous."

"I suppose if they don't return it, I could just gut them?" I asked, knowing this question would elicit a reaction from her.

"What?! No, Kal, we don't go around killing people. Goddess, you AshFieran males and your need for bloodshed."

I smirked over at her briefly before returning my eyes to the road.

She was silent for a moment and then scoffed, "You did that on purpose, didn't you? For a moment, I thought that I was involved with a psycho. Who would just kill anyone on a whim that didn't do what they wanted?"

Shrugging, I answered her, "I have had to do some questionable things in my life, my Enayah. Killing is one of them. And I have killed males for some chaotic reasons. Mostly to extract myself out of situations I didn't care to be in."

"I should have known. Well, remind me to stay on your good side, and if I ever do get on your bad side, just be warned, I don't back down." My beautiful Enayah glanced over and glared, red flaring in those wondrous, hypnotizing eyes.

"I don't believe you would ever get on my bad side. And I am very well aware of your capabilities." I thought back to the competition. She was powerful for someone without shadow-jumping abilities. But no one knew what someone with so much mixed in her blood would be capable of.

A short while later, we pulled up to a massive and well-manicured home. The long driveway was designed to hook around, making it easier for people to come and go. No cars were outside, but I presumed they were in their ridiculously oversized garage—it was almost as big as the house. I stopped the truck under their veranda. A young female stood by the front door, waiting for us to exit, which meant they had been watching for our arrival.

"Wait here, Raine," I said, placing my hand over the top of hers as I gave her a pointed look before exiting the truck and walking around to her side. I wanted to be the gentleman she claimed I was, and opening her door would give me great pleasure.

When I opened the door to let Raine out, she exited, and I placed my hand on her lower back. It gave me delight to touch her so freely. Just a short while ago, I had kept watch over her, unsure if I was allowed to do this. It seemed like such a long time ago already, when in actuality, it had been just a few days ago that I had first introduced myself to this beautiful female.

The female standing in the doorway tilted her head as we approached and spoke directly to Raine, "Hello. You must be Raine, and you must be her companion. We have been awaiting your arrival. If you follow me, I will take you through the house to the back gardens where the Mistress and Master sit."

The female turned around, walking ahead of us, guiding us through the lavish home. On either side of the foyer we entered, a set of stairs led up to a second floor. The prickling sensation of being watched intensified as we approached the hallway under the balcony at the top of those stairs. Quickly glancing upwards, I saw that no one was present. However, I still felt those eyes penetrating Raine and me. And as the balcony disappeared, so did the watchful feeling.

It was a short walk, as we made our way through the hallway that opened onto a small back entryway. On the far side, a set of glass double doors led us out. As we left the back of the home, Raine let out a small squeak that had me immediately halting our movement. Looking around quickly, she blushed, "Sorry, I didn't mean for that to come out, but look at this place. It's–wow. I can't put into words the beauty and energy this place gives off. It's amazing."

Nodding, I glanced back over to the female, patiently waiting for us to continue to follow her.

Walking down a winding brick path, flowers of every color lined up on either side. Raine was still studying her surroundings when we found an open area in the lush gardens. In the center of the brick patio stood an ornate table under a covered pavilion, adorned with flowering vines that ran along the posts and railings. At the table sat a female and a male who looked old enough to be Raine's parents.

The female stood first as we approached. The male raised reluctantly as an afterthought. While the male kept his narrowed gaze on Raine, the female spoke first. "Welcome to our home, Raine and Kalpheus." I gaped at the female. *How in the world did she know my full name?*

"I am a seer, Kalpheus, among other things." She inclined her head. I was sure those 'other things' were mind-reading. They were rare amongst both the AshFierans and Humans. So, it was startling to be in her presence.

"Let us get introductions out of the way. My name is Maggie, and this is my brother, Marcus. Now, let us sit and listen to what you have to say, darling." She said, turning her attention back to Raine.

We sat across from the two of them. Raine was picking at her fingers while regarding our hosts before she spoke, "I'm sure you already know why I am here, Maggie. Gigi said she spoke to someone late last night about the book. So,

I have come here to ask for it back. My mother is being held against her will by my father at our home. I need to get her out of AshFiera and back to Lunaris Falls. And then I need to permanently close the portals between worlds when I have accomplished saving her."

"Hmm, I see." She tapped the table before trifling with a napkin and continued, "I *do* see the need for the book in partial, but why doesn't the shadow-jumper take you back to AshFiera himself?" She questioned, looking back over to me.

"I thought you were a seer?" I retorted.

"Yes, that I am. But I can only see so far when someone has been pushed into my path. You and Raine were pushed into it when my dear friend Gwenmyra called me."

There wasn't a lot of information on seers and their abilities, so I would have to take her word for it. "I can't jump at the moment. Another assassin attacked me, and he had a blade dipped with a drug known to inhibit someone from jumping. Raine's Uncle doesn't know how long it will take to leave my system." I peered over at Raine for a moment, watching her continue to fidget, grabbing her hand under the table. I squeezed it and resumed my explanation, "Raine just found out her mother is alive, and we must rescue her as soon as possible. Especially with her father's hired assassins out there searching for her."

Maggie, the female, remained silent for a while. Her gaze drifted to Raine, becoming unfocused as her eyes glazed over to a white hue. She sat this way for a moment, the glaze cleared, and her full attention was back on Raine.

"I will retrieve your book." She said, snapping her fingers. A young male appeared in the garden's path, heading toward the table, stopping a few feet away. Her gaze was still glued to Raine, "You will have a difficult choice to make in a few days, Raine. Know that whichever one you choose will be the most complicated. Ultimately, it is the correct choice, no matter who protests." Maggie said, glancing at me briefly. "Now, I would like to introduce my nephew, Theo, to you. He has been the keeper of your family's book for the past year."

The young male stepped forward and bowed, reaching out a hand to Raine. She took his hand to shake it, but he brought it up to his lips, giving her a seductive look as he kissed the back of her palm.

I was glaring at the newcomer. My anger elevated with his forward touching. And a growl escaped my lips.

He gave me an askant glance before letting his hand drop, drawing his attention back to my Enayah. She could feel the shift in my demeanor, and with her hand still held in mine, she squeezed lightly.

She spoke to the bold male, "It is nice to meet you, Theo. I'm Raine, and this is Kal."

"Raine, what a beautiful name for an even more alluring woman." His compliment made Raine blush. She squeezed my hand again for reassurance that she was here with me or to restrain me; I wasn't sure. Her touch kept me from killing the male, though.

"Hmm, Maggie says you have my book. If you will please hand it over, we can hit the road and be out of your hair. I wouldn't want to impose any more than we already have."

The male, Theo, smirked before responding, "It will be a pleasure to return this to you, Raine. However, if I may, I would like to take you for a walk through the gardens. Alone, of course." His gaze furrowed when he glanced at me. "It would be good for you to listen to a bit of the history concerning your family. There might be some useful information for you to utilize in your journey back to the shadow realm that would otherwise not be written in the book." His smile towards her was polite, yet it held something hidden behind it.

"I suppose it doesn't hurt to understand a bit more about my family's history. I should warn you, Theo, and I apologize if I sound rude here. But I am trusting you not to lead me astray. I am powerful. Hell, just the other night, I fought a bunch of human men, laying their asses on the floor. That includes the shadow-jumper sitting next to me. I presume you know how strong they are compared to the men here on Earth?" Her boldness caused the male, Marcus, to scoff and the other male, Theo, to chuckle.

"You have nothing to worry about, Raine. It's just a walk and a brief lesson. Nothing more; I will be a gentleman and keep my hands to myself." He placed his hands behind his back to show he meant it literally.

She turned back to me, "Will you be okay waiting for me out here? I would hate to leave you, but I would like to see what he has to say."

"Yes, my Enayah. I will be fine in the company of Maggie and Marcus." I smiled tentatively, making sure she didn't second-guess going away with this male, although I really didn't want her to. She needed the answers, and he would give them.

Raine stood from her chair, walking the short distance to Theo's side. I kept my gaze fixated on her body as they walked towards another path until they turned a corner, where thick, lush plants devoured my view.

Turning back around, I caught the snarl on Marcus' face as he glared at me. Maggie sighed next to Marcus and kicked one of his feet under the table with hers. Causing him to sever his connection with me as he examined her face and what she had done. "Enough, Marcus, you agreed to behave, and I will not tolerate a pissing match in my home."

"My apologies, sister. You know how I feel about the others in his world. It is difficult to sit here with one of them when you know what happened with Pandora." It was the first time he had spoken since Raine and I arrived. He piqued my interest when he mentioned Raine's mother.

"I can assure you I had nothing to do with anything regarding her mother. Pandora hired me through mutual friends to watch over her daughter and keep her safe when the time came. I understand it was not Pandora I kept safe, but I am here to help bring her home at the end of the day."

His eyes lit with anger, and he stood abruptly from his chair. "It does not matter. You are just like the others, taking what doesn't belong to you. First, it was Raine's father taking Pandora, and now it is you trying to take and control the girl. She must seek your approval before taking any action independently. Pathetic." The sneer on his face made him look much older than I had previously thought, but I couldn't fault him for being angry. There was more to him and what happened between Raine's mother than I knew.

"Marcus! I told you to behave. Kalpheus is our guest, and I would appreciate it if you would refrain from speaking to him in such a manner. He has done nothing and doesn't understand our family's history with hers. You need to leave, NOW!" Maggie stood from her chair, chastising the male. He scrutinized his sister briefly before stomping off like a toddler.

"My apologies, Kalpheus. He still harbors resentment for not stopping Pandora from using her family's book years ago. He blames himself for pushing her into running. I suppose this is all confusing without giving you the whole story." She sat back down and folded a napkin across her lap before grabbing the cup from the table and sipping.

"Marcus and Pandora were engaged. It has been a long tradition in certain families that if a man and woman were born in the same year and month, they were to be joined. The marriage would produce the strongest magical children. It hadn't happened in decades until Marcus and Pandora were born. He was over the moon for Pandora from the start, but she was a free spirit. Drifting in our world, refusing to let anything tie her down." She ceased for a bit to take another sip.

"One day, Pandora decided she no longer wanted to abide by tradition or fate and ran. It left Marcus heartbroken, but he never gave up on her. So he chased after her. That's when he came upon her in her living room with the book, he hopelessly watched as she was sucked into the portal. Until that happened, I hadn't developed my seer abilities yet. But when she traveled to the other world, they snapped into place. I had a vision of her future. It broke my heart to tell my brother he needed to move on. Because I saw his future as well, and knowing another path would be presented to him, ultimately led me to envision my nephew's future. All before the motions were finalized." She inspected the gardens, where Raine and Theo had vanished.

"Tell me, do you see her future?" I asked because I needed to know if she would remain safe by my side, not whether I would be in it, but if I was further dooming her to a future of running.

"Bits and pieces, hers are clouded in areas and more complex than I have ever envisioned. I am guessing that is not what you are asking. Do you want to know where you stand in Raine's future? I know you love her, Kalpheus. It is plain to see for anyone with eyes. That is why Marcus is acting belligerent toward you. He thinks you are trying to steal his son's future with Raine."

That caught my attention, "What do you mean by his future with Raine? She doesn't know his son. And I believe if she is anything like her mother, she will not want to be forced against her wishes."

"Oh, I know she is like her mother, that is guaranteed. I see that much, at least." She tapped the side of her head, "And while I agree with you that she doesn't know him, he also plays a part in her future. But both of your futures are far more intimately entangled. It angers Marcus because they were born the same year and month, and he believes that automatically gives his son the right over her. However, he overlooks a crucial part of the family lore: she wasn't born here. In tradition, each person must be born here for it to be a true fateful binding. I wouldn't worry too much since I have the final say anyway. Theo and Raine's fates are entwined, just not how Marcus wants them to be. It will become clearer over time. I cannot divulge any more information. I have to avoid those futures from changing."

As our conversation was coming to an end, Raine and Theo emerged from the gardens. Walking over to the table, she held the book tightly to her chest and beamed brightly when she caught my stare.

"Thank you so much for allowing us into your home, Maggie. I apologize for grabbing and running, but we need to get moving. It's best not to wait any longer to reach my mother." She glanced back over her shoulder. "And Theo, thank you again for the walk and the lesson. I appreciate you keeping this safe for my family."

"It was my pleasure and duty, Raine. Please don't ever

hesitate. I am just a call away if you need any assistance." His eyes gleamed, radiating the lust that was evident while his attention was on Raine.

I cleared my throat and stood, placing an arm low around her waist and pulling her close to my side. I looked toward the female and said, "Maggie, it was an honor speaking with you. Thank you for keeping me company."

She smiled at both Raine and me, "Happy to help. Raine, please tell your mother that I expect her to visit me when she gets back. I promise to have Marcus occupied elsewhere when she arrives. I miss my best friend and would like to catch up."

The female attendant who escorted us through the house earlier was waiting for us at the edge of the path. We followed quickly, and as we got into the truck, Raine was still gripping the book tightly in her arms.

"You know it's not going to blow away." I teased her.

"I know it's not, Kal. I'm thrilled that we have almost completed everything. You won't like this next part, but we have to go back to Gigi's. We have to enter the same way Mom did all those years ago for me to be tied to closing the portals. Theo said we can leave from any location while in AshFiera. But the original spell she used has to be followed."

"Hmm, I suppose there is no going around it. Let's stop at my place first, get some rest, and then in the morning, we will head over." I suggested spending a little more time with my Enayah before we returned to AshFiera, where we might run into her father.

"Sounds good. We have to clean up Gigi's first anyway, and I don't have the energy to do that tonight. I don't want her walking into the disaster those assholes left."

Leaning over the center console, I pulled Raine toward

me. I didn't want to wait for the two-hour drive before I could feel her lips on mine again.

Crushing my lips against hers, I took possession of the moans she let out. It wasn't nearly long enough when I pulled back and licked her bottom lip before adjusting myself in the seat, readying to drive.

The ride back would be far too long, and I longed to strip her naked, worshiping her body and imprinting myself in her pleasures.

Chapter Fourteen
Raine

I was walking away from the table with Theo and away from Kal. He seemed at ease with the whole situation of us coming here. Which, in return, helped me relax a little in the presence of unknown, masterful people.

Theo hadn't spoken yet. I'm guessing he knows Kal had some insane hearing and wanted to be further away before telling me what he was so eager to get me alone for.

The winding path we walked along was made of bricks. While lush flowers encased the sides, giving off different aromas that mingled around my nose. I detected soft, powdery sweetness with hints of cream from several plants, and then others with hints of spice mixed in.

As we continued to walk further along, a subtle tingling in the nape of my neck began to intensify. It wasn't unpleasant, and I recognized the power and serenity as the volume of crashing water increased with the sensations as we approached a waterfall.

It wasn't just any waterfall, though. It mirrored the one I loved to lounge by with Beauty back home. It was so similar that it hid a lake beneath the surface. I looked over at

Theo and caught him watching me intently, his expression one of longing. At that moment, he meant for me to see his gaze.

I stood a few feet away, crossing my arms as I surveyed him. He was attractive. I couldn't deny that. I assumed he was the same age as me, unlike Kal, whom I took to be older. Age didn't matter to me, however. And he was the total opposite of Kal. Who was the typical tall, dark, and handsome, with an emphasis on the mysterious darkness that could suck you into oblivion.

Theo was also tall but exuded sunshine. He had short, golden, wavy hair and cerulean eyes that matched the sky on a clear summer day. Something drew me to him, but it wasn't like how I felt with Kal. What I had with him was all-consuming; I couldn't be away and needed to touch him to recenter myself and feel complete. With Theo, it was more spiritual, and there was an underlying understanding. I didn't think he felt that way toward me, however. I saw those lusty looks as he perused the length of my body. He didn't hide his gawking and only made me tap my foot impatiently, waiting for him to start.

We sat in silence for so long that his voice startled me out of my observations, "I wish for us to be friends, Raine, and well, for that to happen, wouldn't it be grand to tell me a little about yourself?" He coyly asked. I assumed he was curious about the girl who was half witch, half AshFieran.

As far as I knew, I was the only person with my background. If shadow-jumpers had come to the human realm, they would never have had relations with humans. It was taboo due to the significant disparity in strength. My father didn't care, though. He fell head over heels for my witchy mother. Something about her carefree attitude and, most likely, the fact that she had powers drew him instantly toward her.

I answered as little as possible without being rude, "I'm not sure where to begin. I assume you already know my mother's story since Maggie and Gigi talk regularly." He nodded in agreement, "I'm an only child. My father trained me to fight at a very young age, and I kept it up after his 'disappearance' until one day when assassins came and hurt my mother and then tried to take me. Now I'm here trying to get her back and some semblance of normalcy in my life."

"You have had quite the beginning. It will get better over time. Especially with this," Theo presented my family's book out of thin air and held it up for me to view. "I do not wish to hold this from you, but I must tell you everything you need to know before I allow it to leave my hands. My aunt told me a few things that would happen. I can not tell you plainly, as it would defeat the purpose of the future, and I'm afraid it would be rewritten. But I can explain some of the tools you may find useful when the time comes."

I unfolded my arms, letting them relax as I was ready to take it all in. "You have my undivided attention, Theo. Anything that will help me. Even if I must solve the riddles you give me, piece by piece."

"I have no doubt, you are gifted in many ways, Raine. Beauty and brains, *love*. You have both. Did you know that waterfalls are important in a witch or warlock's life?" I shook my head, "They are quite remarkable, just like you. They have an unending natural energy that helps fuel anything nearby. Take, for instance, the flowers and trees here are thriving and in abundance because the falls feed them."

"Okay, but what does that have to do with the importance of a witch or warlock? It feeds the flora nearby, but what does it do for a person?" I asked, getting ahead of our conversation.

"I was getting there," he chuckled. "What the falls do for us is that if one were on the brink of death with our powers drained, it keeps us from that brink of darkness or light, depending on the person's life choices. Replenishing enough to achieve safety. It can also occasionally help bring forth untapped or hidden powers to aid in times of need."

He gave me a pointed look as he shared the last bit of information. Interesting, I thought back to when I was falling over the edge, and suddenly a portal appeared.

That explained how I created the portal to access the human realm. I knew most of what he told me from the stories my mother would tell. Now, I had more questions about how to use this information in the future, but that would have to wait for another time.

"Thank you for explaining the significance. I was always drawn to the falls near my home. They weren't lush like the gardens here, but now I understand why the Ashix were drawn to them."

"Interesting. I am curious since I know little about your home, but what is an Ashix?"

I grinned widely at him, thinking of my fiercely beautiful companion. "My mom said they are similar to your ancient mythical dragons. Except they are smaller, but still absolutely destructive. I have a beautiful female who took a liking to me. They are completely wild, though, so Mom always said I was blessed by the Goddess."

"Fascinating, I would have loved to witness one in the flesh. But once you close the portals, there will be no traveling between worlds anymore. I hope you understand that."

The smile fell from my face. Why didn't I think of

that? I knew I needed to close the portals, but would I lose Beauty forever? I wouldn't even think of bringing her here. It would be chaotic, and she would get lonely if she could never have a life-mate. When we returned to AshFiera, I hoped I would be able to revisit her one last time before I had to say goodbye. It would be challenging, but it had to happen. I needed to remember she was a wild beast that roamed the shadow realm, and it had to stay that way.

Theo was observant as he stepped forward, reaching his hand to tuck a stray curl behind my ear, "I fear your vibrations have shifted. I didn't mean to cause you such sadness."

"No, it's okay. I need to understand the ramifications of my actions now rather than later. Otherwise, I'm afraid I might not make the right decisions." I whispered, swallowing a lump.

Theo was so close to me that the heat radiated off his body and wrapped around mine. He wasn't touching me, but it felt tender. I tilted my head up to look into his eyes, his face slowly moving closer to mine. I realized he was going to kiss me when he licked his lips and eyed mine. I jerked back.

"Theo, I'm sorry if I gave you the wrong impression, but I'm here with Kal. We are only here to retrieve what rightfully belongs to my family and nothing more."

He straightened and gave me a wistful smile. "My apologies. The ambiance of the gardens is almost whimsical and enchanting. I couldn't help myself in the face of beauty."

Blowing out a breath, I took a small step back and held out my hand. It was a silent request for Theo to hand over the book. Reluctantly, he placed it in my palm and let it go. I started to turn, needing to gain some distance from his longing gaze, when his hand shot out, grabbing hold of my forearm.

"Before we return, please let me explain the next part to you. It's the most important if you truly wish to close access between the light and shadow realms."

"Alright, hit me with what you got."

He let go and ran that hand through his hair, "When you read from the book, you must be in the same spot your mother was all those years ago. It will link you with the same vibrancy. Then, you can port out from anywhere in the realm to get back here. Once you return, you must read the same scripture but add 'I command thee closed' at the end and snap your fingers together. I have marked the book where the inscription is located and wrote the ending on a separate note."

"Thank you, Theo. I appreciate you taking the time to help us." And I really meant it; without his help and that of his aunt, we wouldn't be where we are, about to help retrieve my mother.

He gave me a dampened smile and ushered us towards the patio where his Aunt and Kal were waiting. I looked next to Maggie and discovered that Theo's father had disappeared. It made me wonder if something happened while we were away.

Our goodbyes were short, and I could feel Kal's resolve slipping when Theo didn't hide his attraction to me. It caused Kal to devour my mouth before we hit the road. He left me panting and aching all the way home.

Chapter Fifteen

Raine

It was dark out by the time we returned to Kal's. He stopped the truck in front of the porch steps, silently leaving. Most of the ride was quiet, aside from flipping pages as I looked through the ancestral book.

Kal walked around the front, keeping his eyes on mine as he approached my door and opened it with purpose. Reaching a hand toward me, I took it and let him guide me into the house.

When we entered, I walked ahead of Kal—placing the book on the small end table next to the couch. Turning to find where he had walked to, I realized he didn't go too far. He was leaning his body against the doorway to his bedroom. He observed my movements near the couch with an almost hungry gaze. He devoured me with his eyes. I wanted him to devour me with more, and I wanted him to eat up the distance between us.

"Kal, are you okay? What's going through your mind right now?"

My voice broke whatever silent spell he had been

under. He immediately closed the distance between us just as I had wanted.

Wrapping his hands around my waist, he pulled me to his body. I let myself rub against him in a teasing friction. I was abruptly lifted and placed over his shoulder as he made his way back toward the bedroom. He gently laid my body on the bed while I gazed up at him and watched the hunger in his eyes churn.

I had never had a male look at me the way he was at that moment.

Kal draped his body over mine to seize my mouth in a teasing kiss before moving his lips down my neck. His hands slid up my stomach, taking my shirt along with them.

Moving his body off mine, he helped bring my top up and over my head, exposing my bare breasts to the cool room. I laid back, watching his half-lidded eyes take my naked upper half in.

He let out a low, throaty growl before he took a nipple into his mouth. Sucking lightly before popping off and nipping at the tip, then moving on to the next one. He lavished each breast equally, drawing the curling heat moving down to my clit. My body moved on its own as I ground myself on the leg he pushed up against my center. I was so close, but then Kal moved his leg, and I let out a whimper.

"Shh, be a good girl Enayah. Hold still until I tell you otherwise." His command made me let out a whine, which elicited a lusty grin spreading across his face.

Ever so slowly, he kissed his way from my nipples to the underside of my breasts. Down to the middle of my stomach until he reached my navel, biting the skin below the dip of it. He hooked his index and middle fingers into the waistband of my leggings and pulled downward, taking my panties along with them and tossing them somewhere in the room. My body was entirely bare for him, and I shivered. His eyes roved over my form, and I could feel the blush rush in my face and down my chest and body. The vulnerability began to set in, and I went to cover myself when he wrapped his hands in mine, bringing them above my head.

"No, my little star, I wish to look at all of you. Do not hide this beautiful body from me."

I nodded and responded in a whisper, "I'm sorry, it's just that I have never done this before–with anyone."

"No apologies." He hummed, "I do love hearing that I am the only male who has ever touched you. But don't over-think, just feel. If you need to, close your eyes and enjoy every touch, every breath that tickles, and give over your pleasure to me."

So I closed my eyes, helping relax myself into the sensations.

Kal's hands roamed from my waist down to my hips and thighs, stopping at my knees, where he hooked his hands under—pulling my body closer to the edge of the bed, where he kneeled on the floor. He slowly spread my legs wide to fit his broad shoulders in between.

Nothing was happening; I opened my eyes to stare at where he was. His eyes were focused on my center. They began to darken with hunger before he gazed back up at me. Keeping them connected to mine, he moved in, breathing hot air onto my clit.

Moaning, I tilted my head back on the bed as anticipation built before I felt the warm wetness of his tongue exploring my opening up to the sensitive bundle.

When he reached my clit he rolled his tongue around before sucking it into his mouth. I lifted my lower half off the bed, seeking more as my moans increased. Louder and louder, he continued his languished assault. A moment later, I felt the tip of his finger glide into my opening, thrusting slowly in and out while his tongue continued its ministrations.

He added a second finger, enhancing the feeling of fullness. I was so close and needed him to speed up his lazy motions. "Faster, Kal. Yes, I'm almost–there."

"Come for me, Enayah. I want to drink your essence." He growled against my pussy, causing pinprick vibrations. Soon enough, I burst, and a breathy moan escaped my throat as the orgasm consumed me. Leaving me in a pliant puddle on the bed. Kal gently removed his fingers and continued licking up my release, causing little shocks. The oversensitized sensations jolted in my clit while he was still lapping at my wetness, making me push his head away.

Breathing heavily, I looked up at the ceiling, feeling boneless. "Kal, you make me feel so uncontrolled."

"That's the point, my little star. To lose control and give into pleasure." He said, getting up on the bed, and pulling me with him.

I looked at him and reached for his pants. "What about you?"

He stopped my movements, shaking his head, "I already took my pleasure. It was enough listening to you enjoy yourself."

Humming, I turned to my side, draping my leg over his while I laid an arm over his stomach. My head nestled into the crook of his arm, and I took in a deep breath, letting the manliness in his scent relax me beyond the orgasm he just gave.

"Sleep, sweet little star. We have a lot to do tomorrow." He whispered into my hair.

Closing my eyes, I lay still, letting my body relax, turning my wakefulness into a dream-filled memory.

*"F*ATHER*! W*ATCH ME*!" I yelled over my shoulder, hoping Father would witness what I was about to show him next. I held my hand toward the training dummy hanging on a post before me. It exploded right in front of my eyes when I concentrated on the sensations at my fingertips. I whooped a loud cheer while doing a little dance.*

Turning to look behind me, I saw my father grinning from ear to ear. "My little Ashix! You are doing wonderfully, my dear. Your powers are getting stronger every day."

Hearing my father's awe gave me so much joy that I couldn't help but develop a wide smile. Lately, he had been less angry with me and given me more praise and encourage-ment, which I couldn't help but bask in the happiness it gave.

"I'm so proud of you, my fierce little Raine. When your shadow-jumping abilities develop, you will go far as a Shadow Assassin. It shouldn't be much longer now. You are growing into a—what did your mother call it?" He paused, tapping a finger on his chin. "Ah, yes, a fine young woman."

All I strived to do was make him proud, and he uttered those words freely to me. I was drifting on the clouds, happy as an Ashix who took its first flight among the treetops.

"Come, my daughter. We will meet with a friend of mine and go hunting."

Sadness immediately took over, and the smile dropped from my face. I hated hunting for meat if I was the one doing the killing. I could swear every death I took carved a small piece of my happiness from within. Luckily, my father didn't make me hunt too often at my mother's behest. She would always scold him when she found out he took me out into the forest.

My mother wasn't home today. It was a delivery day at the village, so Uncle Cassius took her in my stead. She wouldn't be here to interfere, and I couldn't protest unless I wanted to face his wrath.

Just then, as if my father's will summoned him, an older male shadow-jumped in along with a younger male who had to be a few years older than me. I stepped back and found my father walking up to the two with a grin. "Tesus, my friend, so glad you could make it. I see you have brought your son Zynas. It is great to see he has finally come into his abilities." He turned to the young male, "I look forward to seeing how you have developed your skills."

Father beckoned me to come forth and join in the conversation, "Come, my little Ashix, meet our guests."

I smiled tentatively and slowly walked over next to my father's side. I was looking at the young male in front of me. He donned a smile on his face as he watched me examine him. His smile turned brighter the longer I looked, and he squinted his eyes, making it hard to see the color. But I couldn't mistake the bright honey gold flecks that reminded me so much of mine and my mother's highlights in the summertime. His chestnut hair tied into a bun on the top of his head made me giggle, wondering why a male would have such long hair.

"What's so funny, Raine?" Father asked, and my laughter died immediately.

"I'm sorry, Father. I have never seen a male with long hair before. I would think he was a female if he wasn't so

muscular." I replied with my head down and eyes on the ground.

There was a boom of laughter from the older male, "See, Zynas, I told you females don't like young males with longer hair. It's lucky you are nearing seventeen and have started to develop like a true male."

Zynas glared at me, "Would it please you, Raine, if I cut my hair before the next time we see each other?"

Looking up, I frowned back at him, confused why he would ask me such a thing. "It's not my hair, and it's certainly not my decision what you do with it." At that moment, Father cleared his throat, "Father? Am–am I missing something? I don't understand what's going on. I thought we were going hunting?"

Father placed his hand on my shoulder, turning me to look directly at him, "We are going hunting soon. I want you to take this excursion to get to know Zynas. His father, here, Tesus, is not just a friend but the leader of AshFiera. As I am your father and his second in command, we have decreed that you and Zynas shall be betrothed."

I whipped myself out of his hold, staring at him with betrayal. The fact that, as I grew older, I wouldn't be free to choose who I loved. And at this very moment, he was already deciding my fate so young. "Father, I'm only twelve, nearing thirteen! I'm still a child, and I don't look at males in such a way yet. Don't I have a say in who my future mate will be when the time comes?"

His anger was evident as his voice laced with a low, dangerous growl, telling me I was already in deep and to keep my mouth shut, "You will do as you are told. I will not listen to another word of protest on the matter. You and Zynas will not bind your lives together until after your nineteenth birthday. Until then, we will be spending more time *together, including training. Now, apologize to your future husband for your outburst."*

Seething, I turned towards Zynas, "Sorry for laughing at your hair. I don't give a shit what you do with it."

"Raine! Watch your tongue," Father scolded me.

I rolled my eyes and walked away to grab my bow and arrow, knowing I wouldn't escape this predicament. Whatever my father said was usually the law and would be obeyed.

"Apologies, Tesus. My daughter is nearing her teenage years, and you know females are more temperamental than males." Father had said, not concealing his disdain for my budding attitude.

Tesus flapped his hands, brushing off my actions and words, "No worries, dear friend. I see it so often with the young females who come through Ozryn. They are no different. Zynas will be able to handle her."

Handle me? Surely they were so delusional in this whole betrothal aspect that they couldn't consider my emotions. To them, I was just a silly little female.

Father and Tesus walked ahead, and I started following, not paying attention to Zynas's location until he walked up next to me. I didn't say a word for the longest time. But I couldn't handle the silence with him anymore. "Tell me, Zynas, are you okay with our father's decisions? I'm sure you have some feelings on the matter."

"I don't have a choice, as you know. My father is a leader. Yours is his most trusted friend. One day, when my father dies or is tired of ruling, I will become the next leader. I will need to produce heirs, and my father believes that having the daughter of one of his deadliest assassins would make the best partner. They both think we will have strong children

together. Especially with your mother's lineage." He *explained, all while looking ahead.*

"I see. That still doesn't tell me whether you are okay with it. You can be honest with me, Zynas. It won't hurt my feelings. I would prefer to know now if someone hates me so I don't get any false hope of a friendship."

I waited a long while before he decided to answer me.

"I'm not okay with it at our age, but then again, I am because nothing will happen for years." The answer was *both confusing and relatable, as I felt the same way, but I still needed to understand what it meant to him.*

"What do you mean?" I inquired.

"I don't like my choices taken away from me. But if it were to be chosen for me, I would be happy to say that I am glad it's you. I can already tell you have fire in your veins, based on how you stood up to your father. And you made my father laugh by teasing my hair. He is harder to please than yours."

I smiled; I couldn't help it. I thought Zynas would hate me and hold a grudge for something I couldn't control. "I suppose it would be best to get to know one another? We have quite a few years before anything serious happens, but we could start over and be friends."

He stopped, grabbing my free hand, "I would very much like that, Raine. And I promise to chop my hair before our next meeting."

Giggling, I let his hand go, and we continued walking, "You don't have to, Zy. The longer hair will grow on me." And I giggled even harder when he rolled his eyes.

"I like that nickname, Zy. I want you to be the only one to use it." His voice was soft, and I could barely hear what he said. But a heat crept into my face, and he saw it. He knew I heard him, so he gave me an easy grin.

"Raine! Zynas! Hurry, you two. We spotted a single deer." Tesus called out to us, interrupting our small moment together.

Zy and I jogged up to our fathers and peered into the distance where they were pointing. Standing in the field was a single buck, grazing lazily in the tall, reddish grass.

Father came up behind me and took the bow and arrow from my hands. I turned and glared at him, confused about what he was doing. He answered my unspoken question next.

"I want you to use your powers. Hold the buck in place, and then use your lightning to stop its heart."

I let the horror show on my face, *"I don't know if I can do that, Father. You saw what I did to the training dummy. What if I explode the deer? Aren't we hunting for food? There would be nothing left if I used my lightning."*

"Hush, all will be well, daughter. I know you can do it. Show your betrothed what lies beneath the surface."

Zy walked up beside me, grabbing my hand. *"It's okay, Raine. You can do it. You control the amount of voltage that comes out. It's almost like shadow-jumping. You harness it within and then dial it down before letting it go."*

Letting his hand free, reluctantly, I stepped up. Raising my left hand, I willed the air to trap the buck in its spot. Immediately, the animal started to panic, trying to escape my hold. With my right hand, I let the electric bolts begin to form on the tips of my fingers. The crackling was intense and started to burn hot, so I backed off. The scorching hot zaps of my fingers turned to a warm, fuzzy buzz. I let go of the buzz and aimed straight for the deer's heart.

When my power hit the buck, I instantly felt the animals' fear and pain as if it were my reflection.

A scream tore from my throat as I fell to my knees. The

lightning was forgotten when the crippling pain ripped through me and into my own heart.

Zynas was right there holding onto my body. "Kill the animal. Hurry before the link connects them any further."

In the background, I heard the 'thwip' of an arrow being lodged into the air, and shortly after, the pain receded.

I turned further into Zynas' chest, grabbing a hold of his clothing, and sobbing. He ran his hands soothingly through my hair, whispering, "It's okay, little storm, I have you. I'm going to take care of you."

Zynas lifted me off the ground and cradled me close to his chest, speaking forcefully toward my father, "I'm taking her back home and to bed. I will sit with her until you return or her mother arrives."

My father answered after a short pause, "Very well."

One moment, we were near the field, and the next, we were outside my home. Zynas had shadow-jumped with me. I was about to tell him he would get into trouble for jumping with me when my mother said, "Oh my Goddess, Raine! What happened?"

Zy answered her, "Hello, Pandora. Let me get Raine in bed, and I can explain what happened."

I didn't see my mother, but she more than likely nodded her head since we were moving up to my room.

Zy gently deposited me on my bed, removed my shoes, and tucked me under the covers. He said nothing, kissed my temple, and left me alone. I wanted desperately for him to come back and hold me, but all was silent.

Hours later, my mother entered my room with a vial and some water, and my father was close behind her.

"Pandora, my love. You're just going to wipe her memories of today?"

I watched them closely, staying silent. My mother's voice

laced with a deadly tone, "Yes, Lazarus. Do you have any idea what you did today? Raine is closely connected to the fauna, so when she uses her powers on them, a bond forms, and it snaps when the animal dies. Killing a piece of her." She paused to stare at my father, "You are slowly killing our daughter by making her hunt those she is kindred to."

"Fuck, I'm sorry, my love. I didn't understand your insistence on keeping her from hunting. No longer will she go out with me on those excursions."

"Thank you. Now, I need you to leave so I can perform the spell while Raine drinks the vial."

He inclined his head, starting for the door, but paused, talking over his shoulder, "Will she forget Zynas? They connected today, and I would hate for that to start over."

"She will forget the male. He will need to stay away for a while until she recovers."

"Alright, I will tell him he can come by in a few months to meet her again."

He left, and I sat up, looking at my mother. My heart was in agony, not only for the buck but primarily for Zy. "Am I going to forget Zy, Mom?"

"Unfortunately, yes, you will, Raine."

"I don't want to. Zy was so kind to me today, and I'm lucky to have him as my future husband." I softly smiled. Thinking about how delicate he was with me and how he made me feel protected.

"Your future husband? I'm missing something, baby. What's this about?" Mom asked.

I tilted my head, confused, "Dad said that he and Zynas' father, Tesus, arranged for our marriage when I turned nineteen. Goddess, he didn't even tell you, did he?"

She shook her head, "No, baby, he didn't tell me. It's okay because I am going to get you out of it. Don't worry, Uncle Cass and I already have a plan for your father."

"What, Mom? What do you mean? It's okay, I don't mind, Zy." Panic hurled itself up my throat, thinking of anything to placate her. "Plus, before anything happens, I will get to know him better for the next five years."

She didn't say another word; she handed me the vial, urging me to drink it down and chase it with water while she spoke only a few words.

Chapter Sixteen
Raine

My eyes lazily opened as my body sucked itself back out of the dream world. The sun shone brightly through the bedroom window, indicating that morning had arrived. I sat up in bed, ripping the blanket off my hot, sweaty body, and looked over to Kal's side, which was empty.

I frowned as my dream replayed back. It hadn't been a dream but a memory, and 'Patches' was in it. I had aptly called him Zy as if he had already been in my heart. Where had he been all those years while my father had disappeared? He was absent for someone who had cared for me in such a short time.

I shouldn't be angry, but I knew him before the incident at my home. And he never even said a word that he knew me. Was he a monster now and not the sweet teenage boy who carried me back home? Someone who told me they would take care of me, but they never did.

Why would this memory and my feelings for him come back now? I was falling for Kal. I couldn't have feelings for someone else, especially for someone helping my father capture me. It was confusing, but I couldn't help thinking of him even now.

If I saw that bastard again, I would give him a piece of my mind.

Fuck him for abandoning me, and fuck him for helping my father.

But he wasn't the only person I was angry with. My mother took those memories from me. She locked them away in my mind, along with the powers I was becoming increasingly familiar with. Just another thing she had kept hidden from me.

My stomach growled, and I groaned. I needed to pee and eat something. Maybe Kal was downstairs making us breakfast.

Getting out of bed, I found my panties on the floor next to the end and slipped them back on. Walking to the closet where Kal's shirts hung, I grabbed a plain black T-shirt and pulled it over my head. The edge of the clothing landed mid-thigh, and I shrugged. It would have to do for now. I had no idea where half my clothes landed. I was lucky I found my panties at least.

Leaving the bedroom, I walked through the living room, still not seeing Kal anywhere, and into the kitchen.

In one of the cabinets, I clasped onto the handle of a frying pan and placed it on the stove. When I browsed through the fridge yesterday morning, I saw that Kal had fresh eggs. I was starving for some. I loved making them over-easy with a side of toast.

While cooking, I started humming a tune and swaying my hips side to side when I heard a groan behind me. Thinking it was Kal, I turned around with a beaming grin, but it fell when I saw that it wasn't him but Zynas. He was standing there on the other side of the island with a yearning glare. He was still as handsome as I remembered him all those years ago. But I had to remember he was helping my father track me down, which really pissed me off.

"Goddess almighty, what the *fuck* are you doing here? And how the hell did you find me?" I said, glaring at the male who had coincidentally been plaguing my dreams all night.

"I have my ways, Raine. Now, be a good girl and come with me. Your father is getting impatient waiting for you to come home."

"Hmm, how about no. How's that for starters–*Zy*." Letting the nickname slip, I waited for his reaction and needed to know if that dream was indeed a memory. Or if it was something fucked up, my subconscious made up just to screw with me.

He froze, staring at me. *Ah–ha, gotcha bitch.* "Well? Nothing to say. Does the cat have your tongue, *Zy*?"

"So, you remember, little storm?" He said, breathlessly

"Oh, I remember all right. And don't fucking call me that. You don't get to do that, ever. How could you?" The anger in me seethed, and I needed to know his reasoning for helping my father.

"How could I? What little storm?" He said, giving me a seductive grin. His eye sparkled with mischief as his gaze roamed up and down my body. He let out another groan when the only eye he had left landed on my barely covered thighs.

I snapped my fingers to break his perusal, "I said, don't call me that! And how could you up and fucking abandon me all those years? Huh? We promised to be friends, but you broke that promise by never coming back. And now– now you are helping my bastard father to bring me back home? Where he is holding my mother hostage!" I was beginning to shout at him. The anger trickled out. And I was furious; all this time, I had another friend in that world, and he never showed up. I was lonely for years, aside from my mother and Uncle Cass.

"I didn't abandon you. After discovering your father's disappearance, I came to make sure you were alright. Even knowing you didn't remember me. I wanted to be there for you, but your mother forbade me from coming around. She said that it might trigger your memories, and I didn't want you to remember the pain of that day. So I agreed to stay away, but I never fully left you."

"Okay, so a good excuse as excuses go, but that doesn't explain why you are helping him?"

Zynas blew out a breath and took a step toward me. I held up my hand, letting the lightning crackle at my fingertips, "Not another step. I already said I am not coming with you."

He chuckled—it was a heady sound, but then it turned into an alarmingly dangerous laugh, "You will be coming with me, my little storm. And my males will dispose of that filth who has been touching you. It seems that in my conquest to keep the other males away in AshFiera, I missed one. I won't be making that mistake again."

Nostrils flaring, I was shocked, "You are why the males never took up my flirting and turned their attention to me? I thought that something was wrong with me. I thought maybe my heritage was too much for some to overcome. What the *FUCK*, Zy? Goddess, you are a controlling bastard!"

"You sure have a mouth on you now that you are older. Don't you remember what I told you back at the village? Be careful who you talk to like that. As I have said, be a good girl and come with me. I will make sure you are dressed more appropriately before we leave." He eyed my bare legs with desirous interest again.

Fuck him for being attractive with that stupid eye patch, and fuck him for also being a conniving asshole. I needed to help Kal. He was in obvious trouble if what Zynas said was true, and more assassins were around.

I looked over at the front door, trying to determine how quickly I could make it. I knew that Zynas could shadow-jump, but would there be enough time for me to get more space so I could use my wind to hold him in place? I didn't want to use my lightning on him if I could help it. I wasn't in a good spot beside the stove, which was now smoking from my disrupted cooking.

Zy made my decision for me when he moved quickly around the island. He almost had me in his clutches, but I dodged out of the way using my lightning instead of wind in my panic to shove him hard into the hot stove. His roar thundered in the small space, and I zapped him further until his body went limp to the ground.

Scrambling to my feet, I didn't wait or look back to find out if I killed him. I wouldn't be able to live with myself if I did too much to him. Deep down, even though our time together all those years ago was brief, he had been important to me, even if I didn't remember him until now.

Flinging myself out the front door, I stopped at the top of the steps and watched the two males take me in. One was holding tightly to Kal's neck, squeezing, causing him to choke. The other stood off to the side—only a few feet from a pine tree. A plan was forming quickly in my mind. Hopefully, Kal would be quick enough to escape from the assassin's hold before he was electrocuted.

My internal thoughts were interrupted by the one

standing to the side, "Well–well, look at what we have here. Don't worry, female; your father expects you back in one piece. This male here, well, your father asked us to give him special attention. So let's go, don't make me come and retrieve you. I wouldn't want an accident to happen and my hands to go–wandering. Especially since you bear so much delicious skin to touch."

Disgusting piece of trash. No way would I let him get near me. He had no idea what powers I possessed. Maybe Father thought they were still lost since I had never used them during encounters with the other assassins. And I was sure Mom told him she muted them long ago.

Giving the assassin who spoke to me my best 'frightened' look, I said, "Please, don't hurt him. I promise to come with you willingly." I added some eye-batting that I used on Mom in the past to get my way.

He gave me a sly grin, "Ah, so you will play nicely? That's too bad. I was looking forward to handling you personally. Okay, female, you come here, and I will let this peon go."

Oh, I had no doubt he would let him go, just not in the way they were thinking. Taking a few hesitant steps down the stairs, I stopped at the bottom and glanced back up. I hoped my face conveyed the deadly, 'crazy girl' smile. Because I sure felt like it for a moment, I embraced that deep, dark part of myself for what I was about to do next.

Flinging my arms out in either direction, I quickly guided my hand to hold the bastard who had been speaking in his place. At the same time, the other shot out the barest of lightning, aiming for the other male's arm, which held Kal's throat.

The spark's light began to intensify, causing the jerk who held Kal to drop his arm. Once he was out of the way, I let more lightning free, directing it to the male's heart. His body fell into the grass with a heavy thud, which allowed me to refocus on the other male who was still being held near the trees.

Giving him a wicked smile, I let loose my powers, and he crumpled quickly.

Kal was limping toward me, grabbing my face with his hands. "My Enayah, you're okay. Gods, that fucking poison made me weaker than I thought. I couldn't even fight them off." I was incredibly thankful for those hands that were touching my skin and bringing me back to reality.

"Those bastards didn't know what was coming to them. There's another assassin in the house. I unfortunately know that one, and we have a somewhat complicated history. I hope I didn't kill him like the other two, though."

"A past? Is this something I should know about?" Kal asked.

Chewing on my lip, I hesitated to tell him, but I needed him to understand who this other male was. I felt our fates were further entwined, and I wasn't sure if it could be avoided. My instincts screamed this was important.

"When I was twelve, my father betrothed me to Zynas. He's the leader, Tesus's son. I received the news on the same day an incident involving my father occurred. He forced me to use my powers on a deer that hurt me in return. Zy was kind to me, and my soft heart. He brought me back home, and my mother took over my care. She gave me something to make me forget about the incident and Zy."

"Wait? You're betrothed to AshFiera's leader's son?" Kal was putting the pieces together and seemed to be taking it in stride.

"Technically, yes. Back then, I had disagreed with it

until I spent several hours with Zynas, which changed my mind. Today, however, I disagree with it. Zy is not the male I remember, and it hurts that he is helping my father. I learned about it all last night when a memory from my dream surfaced. And then, I confirmed it with Zynas earlier while I was inside making breakfast."

"So, I have some competition for your affections?" He grinned down at me. Shocked by those words, I stared at him. He wasn't angry about the news.

"Kal, I care deeply for you. Every day, it grows stronger. I can't imagine my life without you in it, but I need to be honest with you because deep down, some part of me still cares for Zy. Of course, I don't know him anymore, but I know you, and I'm here with you."

"It's alright, sweet star. I understand. Now, should we go inside and tie Zynas up? Maybe I can beat some information out of him?" He chuckled, rubbing his chin.

Clicking my tongue, I said, "No, you'll not beat him up. I can convince him to talk. We have to be careful he doesn't try shadow-jumping with me. I have an inkling he would take me straight to my father, given the chance."

Kal grabbed my hand and squeezed. Walking back into the house together, we entered the kitchen, abruptly halting in the doorway. "Shit, he fell in front of the stove, that's where I left him. I didn't even look back to see if he was all the way unconscious. I felt guilty enough zapping him and thought I might have killed him."

"It's fine. Zynas is long gone, Raine. He probably went back to your father. We need to get to your grandmother's house and set up the portal."

"You're right. I need to put on more clothes first."

"Mmm, I like you this way, though," Kal said, wrapping

his arms around my body and kissing the side of my neck before letting me go.

I suppressed a laugh. Kal was ridiculous and a pervert. But I liked the way he looked at me even in the simplest attire.

ARRIVING at Gigi's and walking through the door in the daytime was so much different than when we had been here last. The house was more trashed than I thought a few days ago. Glass littered the floor in almost every room as if the assassins relished breaking things just for the fun. Or perhaps it was a message that everything I held dear could be shattered in an instant.

It took hours to sweep and clean everything up. By the time we were done, night had fallen, and the dark shadows danced outside the windows. I stood in the living room, gazing at the pictures on the mantle, and thought back to the day I had arrived.

I was so scared back then, a helpless girl with no clue what the truth had been. My father wanted to use my powers. In what ways, I still didn't understand. My mother lied to me and hid my magic from my father, but I couldn't be angry with her. She did it to protect me, but I needed to hear it from her. I wanted her to tell me that's all she meant it for, and for no other reason.

As I gazed at the pictures, hands covered my waist, and a large body pressed against my back. Kal bent his face into my neck and took a deep breath—the whisper of air as he exhaled titillated goosebumps down my body.

Turning in his grasp, placing both my hands on his

chest, pushing lightly so he backed up to where I wanted him to go. The back of his legs bumped into the couch, and I pushed harder, making him fall on his ass.

Climbing into his lap, I kissed him deeply. And a groan left his lips while his hands gripped my thighs, sliding up to my behind. I pulled back and grabbed the bottom of his shirt, pulling it off. Getting the perfect view of his tattooed chest, I scraped my nails down, leaving shallow red streaks.

Tenderly kissing each mark I left on him, I gazed into his eyes, "I want you inside me, Kal. I want to feel you in all ways."

"Oh, my little star, it would be my delight to give you more pleasure than you could imagine. If we do this, you will be mine, and I will be yours. There is no going back because once I have you, I won't be able to let you go."

Nodding, I mustered up the courage and ripped the shirt from my body, ready to give all of myself to him. He lifted me in the air and gently laid me on the floor in front of the fireplace, placing himself between my thighs. A sigh left my throat as I relished his broad body over mine.

Kissing me softly, he took his time, languishing on my lips. Opening my mouth in a moan, he swiped his tongue against mine. A soft breath escaped as the awareness of a pulse began to ascend down my belly and into my center.

Kal sat up, slowly sliding my bottoms off my hips, discarding his pants in the process. His already hard cock jerked at my exploring gaze, and I licked my lips, a bead of pre-cum formed at the tip like a beacon of welcoming want.

Before he could move back over my body, I sat up and bent forward, licking the head. His cock was warm and had hints of salty musk. Sucking his length into my mouth, I let him hit the back of my throat before gagging. His cock barely fit in my mouth; he was immensely long and thick.

Even encasing my hand around his base, there was still more of him not covered by either my mouth or hand.

He groaned above me, "Fuck–that pretty little mouth feels so good, Raine."

Humming in agreement, I continued to suck and lick around the head. Gathering up my spit on his length, squeezing my hand, and pumping a few times before he moved out of my reach.

"No more. I need to be inside you. Are you ready for me, little star? Is this cunt wet?" His words were crude but made my arousal spiral further.

I didn't have time to answer before his fingers probed my core. He pushed one digit in. I could hear the wet suction as he began moving it back and forth. My cheeks heated at the sound, and I was embarrassed, but I was distracted when he added a second finger. A moan left my throat. I already felt so full that I didn't know if I could take his thick length; his cock was larger than his fingers.

"That's it. You are so wet for me. Now relax this pretty pussy."

His fingers continued pushing in and out, his thumb rubbing circles around my clit, and my climax slammed into me like crashing waves of ecstasy.

"Yes! Ahh!"

Kal's movements slowed while he eased his fingers out and sucked them into his mouth. He took his time to clean them before he moved his body between my thighs.

With one hand on the floor next to my head, the other was gripping his throbbing cock. He pumped once, twice, and lined the tip to my center, pushing himself into my core. Slowly, he inched his way in, thrusting with shallow movements, stopping every little bit to let me adjust to his size.

"Kal, yes. Oh, Goddess, you're big. I'm so full."

"Almost there, beautiful. You are taking me so nicely." He said, gritting his teeth while he continued to pulse little by little inside.

With the last thrust, he ripped right through my barrier, and I was no longer a virgin. I was his, and he was mine. The pain subsided, and all that was left was wanton need. And I needed him to move.

"Good girl, Raine. Are you ready for me to move? Once I start, I won't be able to stop."

I nodded, impatience won over the pain I had felt earlier, "Yes, please move. I need you to move, I'm ready."

So he did. His thrusting began slowly until it became all-consuming, demanding my body bring forth another orgasm. I gripped his arms tightly, digging my nails deep into his muscles as the rhythm of our bodies danced their exotic tangle.

The coil winding itself, so tight in my stomach, became so taut that I knew I was getting close to the edge again. Needing to crash deep into the pit, I whimpered, "Kal! I'm so close."

"Be a good girl, and come for me, Raine. Give me what I want."

And his command sent me over the precipice. His punishing thrusts prolonged my climax, and I was rushing into one after another.

Kal's movements stopped being rhythmic and became jerky and uneven as he approached his release. He roared to the ceiling when he finally reached the height of his pleasure. His cum warmed my insides as his bucking hips slowed. Our breathing mingled together as he slowed to a stop.

We laid on the floor entangled together, and we didn't

move for a long while as Kal kept himself buried deep within me, breathing heavily into my neck. He touched his forehead to mine and then closed his eyes.

"Gods, I didn't think anything could feel like heaven, but being inside of you is what I imagine it to be like." He breathed out.

Pulling himself out slowly, his cum dripped down my thighs. I wasn't ready for the emptiness he left behind, and I whined when he entirely removed himself.

"I will get you a cloth. Lay there and don't move."

"I don't think I could move even if I wanted to. My legs are like jelly." I giggled, the jittery feeling of the adrenaline coursing through my limbs making them pliable.

I could hear him chuckle in the bathroom, and then a moment later, I felt the wet heat of a cloth gently cleaning my legs and pussy. Hissing when he hit a particularly sore spot, he looked at me in concern. I expected it since it was my first time, and Kal wasn't small.

He glanced at me, concerned, "Are you alright, my Enayah?"

"Of course, nothing I can't handle." My smile faltered as the last remaining jolts from his ministrations ran through me.

He finished quickly, picking me up and carrying me to the bedroom. Placing me on the bed, he slid my body under the covers while joining shortly after. He kissed my shoulder and neck, nuzzling his way into my hair. Seconds later, my ears caught the sound of his even breathing, which told me he was already fast asleep. It only lulled me to sleep right behind him, and good thing too, as tomorrow would be hectic and unpredictable.

Chapter Seventeen
Raine

In the morning, Kal and I focused on moving all the furniture out of the way and against the walls. Anything breakable was packed into a box and placed in a different room for safekeeping.

We didn't know how the portal would work inside the house, but there was no other choice since that was where Mom had created it in the first place. She most likely did that to prevent Marcus from entering the home and stopping her easily. If she had made the portal outside, he would have been able to disrupt her chanting.

Grabbing a piece of white chalk, I formed a circle that would likely prevent the portal from getting too big. The instructions were clear in the spell book: *to open the portal, use chalk, draw a circle, and repeat the incantation.* Closing the portal permanently would be similar, except for a few extra words and snapping my fingers together. It had to be easy enough. Right?

"Okay, I think everything is set. You ready?" Still kneeling on the floor, I looked up at Kal, waiting for his answer. He was frowning at where I drew the circle.

"What's the matter? Does it not look right?" I said, looking down at the floor.

"I'm not sure, Raine. Something doesn't feel right, and I can't put my finger on it."

"Oh, Kal, everything will be fine. We will likely head to the falls, where we can find shelter under the cover of the woods. We can sit still for as long as we need before moving on. But it has to be today. Zy has probably already told Father I have my powers back."

He muttered his displeasure, "Alright if you say so. But, Raine, you *will* listen to me when we arrive in AshFiera. There is no need for you to play the hero and take all my fun."

"I understand. Completely–Anyway, before I read this spell, I'm going to leave Gigi and Aunt Sam a note in case they come home before we make it back here ourselves." The only answer I got from him was a grunt as he continued to check for little knick-knacks I might have missed putting away.

I left the living room and found a pen, paper, and an envelope. Hurriedly writing two letters, I shoved them inside and placed them under a cookie jar. Pulling the glass jar out of its spot, I left enough of the envelope sticking out to catch someone's attention.

Heading back into the living room, I smiled affection- ately at Kal. He was standing with his back facing me by the chalk lines, his legs spread apart, and his hands clasped together. He looked like the assassin and deadly killer I knew he could be. His posture wound tight as if something would jump out at any moment.

Clearing my throat, I approached him, "Now I'm ready. We should move back a bit." Taking a few extra steps away from the chalk-drawn circle, it was time to open the way back home.

The nerves vibrated through my body, leaving little shivers as I lifted the book into my hands. With one hand out in front of my body, my palm facing the fireplace, I began the incantation, *"Darkness beyond the blackest abyss, open wide to swallow us whole, guide us through the passage safely, to the other side that waits."*

Nothing happened, and I blew out a frustrated sigh.

Hands found their way onto my hips, gripping lightly, and the flutter of lips descended to my neck. Rolling my head to the side, I let Kal have better access. His kisses started light like the graze of butterfly wings and grew more demanding. He steadied my body with those rugged hands and squeezed tighter.

The tingling began in the tips of my fingers. And then, a gust of wind blew around the room, whipping my hair into my mouth. Choking on the pieces that flew into it, I spit them out, sputtering my lips together in dramatic fashion.

"Stupid wind. I should have pulled my hair into a bun before I did that."

Kal was obnoxiously laughing behind me, turning I punched his arm as best I could.

"Not funny; maybe I should choke you with my hair and see how you like it."

The moment it was out of my mouth, I smacked a hand to my face, "Don't even say a word. Not one word."

He raised his hands in surrender and looked amused that I made an innuendo and fool of myself.

With the wind still whipping around, I looked up and gasped. When I fell through the first portal I created at the falls, I didn't get to see what it looked like, but standing here, I could examine what I made.

It was almost a perfect oval; the surface rippled like

dark water. I gripped Kal's hand, squeezing him, and pulled him behind me toward the shimmering black abyss.

Engulfing us immediately. The sensations slithered warmth and tingling throughout my entire body. Then we walked out together on the other side, avoiding being spit out like the first time.

"Wow, that's a much better way to come through than the last time." I snickered.

"Of course, it would be Enayah. You were falling into the last one instead of walking upright. Usually, with these kinds of portals, whichever way you go in is how you come out." He said, shrugging as he moved us away from the ledge of the falls.

I realized then that it brought us where I thought it would. Smiling to myself, I internally danced.

Raine-1 Assassin's-0. Eat that, you fucks, because you have no idea what is coming for you!

Examining our surroundings, I concluded that no Ashix were around the falls yet again. That was incredibly odd since it had also been that way before I left. Wondering what spooked the beasts, I headed where Kal had already walked toward, right in the direction of my home, where my mother hopefully was waiting to be rescued. She didn't know yet it would be Kal and me who would come. I'm sure she was waiting for Uncle Cass and his bandwagon of misfits to show up.

Kal stopped at the edge of the woods, ducking down behind a Giant Sequoia and some ferns that bushed out in either direction of the roots. It was the perfect cover and the best view for a good old 'stake out'. He turned to me and put a finger to his lips, indicating to keep quiet. I mimed, taking a key and locking my lips while throwing it away, making Kal smile and shake his head. Then he turned back around to survey the house for any movement.

It wasn't long before several males exited through the front door onto the porch. A handful of the males left and started walking around the property, keeping guard. Two remained on the deck, looking around to examine where the other males had walked off.

I was scouring the windows, waiting to see any movement inside. A moment later, several bodies walked past, but the shadows blended like several males were walking next to each other.

I whispered as low as possible, "Kal, there are too many. I can't count how many are inside, but there's more movement in the house than what came out."

He whispered back to me, "I know. We will sit here as long as it takes. They are bound to leave at some point. I can't imagine that all those Shadow Assassins wouldn't have upcoming jobs they need to attend."

"Shit, I wish I had thought to bring some snacks or something. We're going to get hungry eventually, and knowing my stomach, it likely won't stay quiet." I said, pointing out the fact that I had an actively loud bodily function.

"Don't worry, little star, I spotted a berry bush in that direction," he said, pointing off to the right. I turned my head to glimpse where he was pointing while he continued speaking. "It's full of berries, so we should be good for at least a day. If we have to sit here any longer than, let's say, when the sun rises in the morning, we'll have to leave and retrieve better food before returning."

So we sat hiding in the ferns, watching and waiting until the sun started to descend below the treetops. I was popping a couple of those berries that Kal fetched for me into my mouth when several males exited my home and walked around. They stood out front, talking in a big group. We couldn't catch what they were saying, but then several of them shadow-jumped, disappearing instantly.

I gripped Kal's bicep, and we watched on as only a few males stayed behind. They walked back into the house, leaving only one to guard the front door.

"We need to go now," I said, breathless and anxious to save my mom.

"Just wait; let's make sure they don't return immediately."

"Kal, if we don't go now, they might return and not leave. This is our chance. We need to take it. I can portal out from inside the house, and when everyone is safely in the human realm, I'll close it." I stared at him, waiting for him to listen to my reasoning. I was getting impatient; the sweet victory of saving my mom was within reach, and I would take it with or without him. "If you don't help me, I will do it myself."

He panicked when I started to stand. "Wait–Okay, Raine–Just wait. There's one on the porch. We should lure him away from the house and take him out before we enter and deal with the others. Remember, there might be more than we realize, and you need to be prepared for anything. You got it?"

"I got it! Now let's get my mama back and blow this popsicle joint!"

Before we moved, he gripped the back of my neck, pressing his lips to mine, giving me a brutal, short-lived kiss that left me breathless. "Let's go, my sweet little star. I'll give you a proper kiss when we return to safety."

Running to the left where we had been hiding, we stuck

to the forest until we brought ourselves to the side of the house. Kal made a low, rustling noise, accompanied by a groan. I didn't know if it would work, but the male rounded the corner and headed toward us. We walked further into the woods, forcing the male to come in and investigate, thereby avoiding the view of any watchful eyes from the house.

He didn't know what hit him once Kal attacked. Pulling him into a headlock and squeezing tightly to block the airflow until the male slumped. I approached slowly, keeping my eyes on the male who had his closed, "Is he dead?"

"No, just unconscious. I know this one, and while I thought he was a good male, I can't bring myself to end his life. Don't worry. We'll tie him up. The most he can do is shadow out, hands bound behind his back. It will be harder for him to accomplish since our instincts will want them in front of us, and he won't be able to do that." Kal had grabbed the rope he had attached to his belt and begun wrapping the assassin's wrist tightly.

"Good point. So, we need to discuss what will happen when we enter the house. I thought it might be a good idea for me to go in first, and zap who I can while you back me up."

He glanced at me from the ground, finishing tying up the male, and stared, "No."

I glared at him, slightly shocked but not enough to understand his reasoning when I thought it was a solid plan. "No? Look, I'm the only one with powers at the moment. You can't shadow-jump, and who knows if your strength is fully back yet. We are doing this my way, or you can hit the highway."

"Raine," He said, exasperated, fingers pinching the

bridge of his nose. "There are no highways in AshFiera. That analogy only works on Earth."

"Whatever! Don't care. Seriously, you're going to fight me on this? I'm our best chance of taking out however many unknown males are holed up in my home. You know it, and I know it."

The seconds ticked by, which felt like minutes, when he finally relented, "Fine, you go in first, and I will be your backup. But, when we reach your mom, do the spell, and let's get the fuck out of here."

Squealing, I wrapped my arms around his neck and gave him a quick peck on the lips, bouncing a skip towards the edge of the tree line, waiting for him to join me.

He was with me shortly after finishing tying the male up and hiding him from anyone looking into the woods. And then, we set off in a running sprint to get next to the side of the house, plastering our bodies flat. It was as if I were one of those secret agents in one of the movies Aunt Samara had me watch one evening with her. I was entranced by the stealth they perceived in the movies while I shoved handfuls of popcorn in my mouth.

Peeping my face around the corner, I didn't see anyone in the front. I signaled forward with two fingers, and we moved stealthily up the steps and onto the porch. Quickly grabbing the outer door, I kicked the inner one open. It went crashing into the wall, and inside, hanging out in our foyer, were three soon-to-be electrocuted assholes.

I took the males in giving them a sinister grin before I unleashed the pent-up anger in the form of my lightning. These fuckers would learn not to piss off a half-witch. Their grunts and pained groans filled the room, and one by one, they fell.

Looking back over my shoulder, I beamed brightly, "Told you it was a good–"

The air was suddenly knocked out of my lungs as my body flung across the ground by a male I didn't see coming. He must have come from the living room, and I was stupid enough not to pay attention.

However, Kal was quick to act and pulled the assassin off me, throwing him into the opposite wall that cracked behind him. Coughing to catch my breath, I raised my hand and quickly stopped the attacker's heart with a jolt.

"Raine! Gods, are you okay?"

"Mhm, just peachy. Fuck that guy was a tank." I coughed.

"Raine?" A soft voice asked from the other room. I knew it was my mother and that she was waiting for us. Scrambling to my feet, Kal helped me up the rest of the way. I entered the living room first, with Kal close behind me. My mother was sitting on the couch in the middle of the room. She was as beautiful as the day I last saw her. My father must have been taking good care of her. She didn't have a bruise or scratch anywhere on her.

"Mom! Goddess, you are a beautiful sight to behold."

"Hi, my little Ashix. I am so happy to see you again, but you shouldn't have come. You should have let Cassius figure out how to get me out."

Shock rushed through me along with pain at her chiding, "You knew that Uncle Cass was working on a way to get you out?"

My mother, stricken with shame, said, "I'm sorry, baby. It was part of our plan. If I were ever held against my will, he would gather a group to help rescue me. We came up with many different scenarios in case something went wrong."

"Sorry to say, Mom, but I crashed your plan. Come on, let's get moving. We have a portal to make. This realm can kiss our ass goodbye."

She stood from the couch and walked toward me. That's when I viewed the shackles on her wrists clinking with her movements. "What the fuck are those, Mom?"

"Language, Raine, and these are a gift from your father. He had another witch spell them, so I couldn't use my powers to escape or make his life hell, I suppose." She smiled slightly, but it appeared forced.

"Kal, can you remove them from her wrists?" I said over my shoulder.

Mom looked past me, spotting Kal.

"Hello again. I presume you have been with Raine this whole time?"

Kal nodded and answered her, "Yes, I have been guarding her for the last few months. Although it wasn't until recently that she met me."

I shook my head. "What he means to say is that he was stalking me for a while and then threw himself into my life. It's okay, though, because he sure is easy on the eyes." I said, winking at the handsome male in front of me.

"My Enayah, you can call it stalking, but I call it guarding."

"Yeah, yeah–whatever–anyway, Kal, use that manly strength of yours and break this sucker."

With my command, he stepped up to my mom, reaching toward her wrists. Grasping the shackles in both hands, he quickly crumpled them into pieces that clattered loudly to the floor.

"Well, that was easier than I thought it would be. Either that or your strength came back."

"His strength was gone? What happened while you

were away?" Mom asked, her eyes wide as she looked back and forth.

"A lot happened. You remember that sickly pale male who stopped us outside the village wanting to walk us home?" She nodded. "He was a shadow-jumper and found us at Kal's home. He attacked Kal, injecting him with something that Uncle Cass said mutes their jumping and strength. That was a few days ago. But the rest of my adventures can wait until we are safely on the other side, so it's best we skiddaddle."

I pushed the furniture toward the walls, creating a large area to form the chalk circle and portal. Kal began moving the other furniture that I hadn't reached yet, and I stopped to speak to Mom. "Where is your chalk? I need a piece."

"Let me find one for you. Hold on." She quickly left the living room and entered the foyer. I could hear her scrounging around in a drawer in one of the side tables, and she came back quickly with a small yellow piece.

"That's all you have?" I was suddenly worried; the tiny piece wasn't going to be enough to draw a large enough circle.

"Yes, you're lucky I found this. Looks like your father gathered up what I had in plain sight and disposed of them. He missed one hidden in a folded piece of paper."

"Alright, it's just going to have to do. Thanks."

Quickly, I drew another circle, this one sloppier than my first. The need to rush coursed through me as if something was about to happen if I didn't hurry and leave AshFiera behind. Luckily, that small piece was enough to form a somewhat decent shape.

I stood, looking at my handiwork, and wiped my hands on my leggings. I gazed over at my mom and Kal, who stood next to each other on the other side of the room. I smiled at them. It was time to get the hell out of this house. We were heading back to my new home, where we would finally be safe.

Holding up my hands, I aimed my palms toward the wall where the portal would appear, and I was about to begin the incantation again when I felt it. A shift in my magic as several males appeared in the living room, interrupting our departure.

Welp, it was too late to leave now.

Chapter Eighteen
Raine

Staggering backward from the force of many males entering the living room and surrounding areas, I glanced around—finding my gaze landing on the one male I had so many fond memories of while growing up —the one who had been hunting me and wanted me by his side.

My father.

My eyes scanned the room to every male's face, and none of them I recognized. I didn't see Zy in the mix either, so I was curious about where he was hiding. My mind strayed back to my mother and Kal. I needed to find a way to open the portal and get them to safety along with myself.

My father abruptly interrupted my thoughts, "My little Ashix, there you are." He spread his arms wide, "Well? Are you going to come and give your father a hug? After all, it has been five years since you have seen me, and I have missed you dearly."

"No."

His once smiling face fell at the singular word that left my mouth.

"No? After all I have done to find you? I'm hurt that my favorite daughter wouldn't want to hug her father."

"I'm your only daughter. And why would I want to come near a male who sends assassins to hurt her mother, your mate, might I add? And then attempt to kidnap me at every chance? How was I supposed to know who wanted me? For all I knew, some lunatic was going to kill me or, worse, sell my body for nefarious reasons." Every little scenario had been played and replayed in my mind before I knew who wanted me back in AshFiera.

"My fiery little Ashix, I wouldn't dream of harming you. And the damage that was caused to your mother was purely an accident. The male who touched her is no longer among the living. No one harms what is mine and what I love." His face crossed with a sneer and a faraway look, but that one word he uttered blew my resolve to pieces.

"LOVE? You fucking call this love? Are you delusional? You must be because people don't do this to loved ones. You shackled your mate and held her hostage in her own home." My rage had hit an all-time high, and he was the reason for my rolling emotions. I was ready to leave and get my mom and Kal to safety; it was time to go. "We won't be staying any longer, Father, so if you will excuse me."

I began to turn, but his laughter rang out in the room, "Oh, on the contrary, you are not going anywhere. None of you are. Well, I'll take that back." Glancing toward Kal, his smile grew menacing, "You, Kalpheus, will not be staying. No daughter of mine will be associated with a male like you. Plus, dear daughter, have you forgotten you are betrothed to another? I'm sure Zynas will join us shortly and won't be happy to see you are with another male."

My eyes darted over to Kal, and I silently pleaded with

him for guidance. But his following words dashed my hopes that we would escape this easily.

"There are too many, little star. I can detect more males gathering outside that are surrounding the house." Kal said, answering the silent question he seemed to know I was asking.

Fuck, not good. Not good at all.

"Indeed, you are trapped." Father waved a hand toward the other males. "Go find something useful to do until I am finished here. I would like to have a few words with my daughter." They all herded out the door like good little puppets being manipulated by their master.

Now that the males were gone, the air lightened, and I could breathe easier without so many clashing energies congregating in such a small space.

Father clapped his hands together, startling me, "Perfect, now that it's just us, you can both pack a bag. We are leaving for the capital, and you can come with me willingly, or I can haul you both kicking and screaming. Your choice?"

"Father, if I agree to come with you of my own free will," I began.

"Raine–No!" Mom interrupted, knowing what I was about to offer up before I had even spoken it.

"Hush, my love. Let our daughter finish her thoughts. I would very much like to hear where this is going." Father boomed over her outburst.

Clearing my throat from the clump of emotions, I continued, "If I agree to come with you of my own volition, I want your word that you will let my mother and Kal go freely without harm."

He scratched at his chin as if he were considering my offer, but deep down inside, my instincts screamed he wouldn't take it—at least not the deal with my mother.

"Your mother is not an option. She is mine, and I will not be without her again. But as for Kal." Another dramatic pause filled the room. "No, I have decided he can not live. However, I will give you the mercy of choosing who ends him. Either I do it, and he will suffer because I would enjoy inflicting pain on him. Or you can do it, giving him mercy and ending it quickly."

"What the *fuck* kind of options are those?" I screeched. He was giving me no viable choices where Kal would come out unscathed on the other side.

His deadly glare rooted me in my spot. "Watch your tongue, young lady. Until you bind yourself to Zynas, you will be under my care and protection. I will not tolerate disobedience or foul language."

I looked at Kal, tears blurring my vision. It would be the last time I would see him. Everything we shared, our life, our bodies. It would be wiped away soon. I was warring with myself. The only choice my father gave me was to spare him mercy by doing it myself or cause him pain at his hand.

I stood in the living room, contemplating, when an idea began to form. There was another option that would spare not only Kal's life but also get my mother away from my father. I would be left to deal with the aftermath, of course, but I knew he wouldn't hurt me. At least not badly enough to kill me because he needed me for something more.

Now, I needed to enact that plan. The room was too enclosed, and I hoped my confidence would shine through in such a tight situation. It would be chaotic, but seeing that rage in my father's face would be glorious when he realized what I could do.

Looking up through my eyelashes, playing coy so as not

to draw suspicion. I spoke, "Okay, if Kal is truly to die, then I want to be the one to do it. At least then, I know he will go quickly and find peace that much sooner."

"That's my little Ashix. I knew you would choose wisely. Go on, then; let's get this over. I'm ready to show you your new home and the bedroom I have picked for you in the city mansion. It has a beautiful view of the city on one side and a glorious view of the forest on the other."

Turning toward Kal while keeping my father in my peripheral vision, I locked eyes with him. "Kal, I'm so sorry it has to be this way, but know that you have my heart and always will."

"Enayah–no, please. You know there are other options. You don't have to do this."

I didn't think he was pleading for his life. Did he know what I was going to do? It would devastate both of them. But I would work to reunite with them one day when it was safe and when there wasn't a possibility of my father coming after me or sending his minions.

Before I opened my mouth, my nostrils flared, and my body began struggling to suck in air. Something was happening. It was identical to when Zy directed me to dial my powers back, but it was different, as if my body was being sucked in, disappearing from the spot I stood.

That's when I realized this must be what shadow-jumping was. I would use this to my advantage. So, I embraced it, disappearing from where I was and reappearing behind my father.

I pushed myself further away from my mother, Kal, and the portal location. But it was so worth it because my father was frantically looking for me when he suddenly turned around. His eyes were wide, and his face paled. He started toward me, but I was quicker. I held him in place with my wind, trapping him the same way he made me trap that deer. I wouldn't let him advance any further, but he was fighting me, and I worried he might be able to escape my hold as my magic was still new to me.

Aiming my other hand toward the chalk-drawn circle in the middle of the room, sweat dripping down my temple, gritting my teeth, I recited the spell that I had aptly memorized: *"Darkness beyond the blackest abyss, open wide to swallow us whole, guide us through the passage safely, to the other side that waits."*

Father made a sound between a grunt and a scream, and I faltered slightly, which allowed him to move closer to where I was standing.

The portal formed, whipping wind around the room. Glancing at my mom, I saw tears forming in her eyes. She began to step forward, and I held my hand toward her.

"Please don't make me use it on you. Just go, both of you! I don't know how much longer I can hold him. He's strong." I pleaded, my teeth gnashing together as my father's resistance shook the grasp I had on him.

"No, I won't leave without you, Raine." My mom wept.

Then, my eyes drifted to Kal. It was evident he was furious. It hadn't been part of the plan, and he knew I would sacrifice myself to save my mother and his life.

"Get in the fucking portal." I hissed through my teeth.

He shook his head and started for me. With my hand still raised, I easily focused my powers on the wind. The invisible force cascaded around both my mother and Kal in a loving embrace. Anything that wasn't weighed down started floating around the room, crashing into walls and furniture as I intensified the flow. I needed to push a bit harder to get their bodies moving.

There would only be seconds before I had to let go of my father. The energy was draining from me fast. As lethargy settled into my limbs, it became increasingly more challenging to hold them up.

With one last peek at Kal, I uttered the only remaining words I wanted him to remember, "I love you, Kalpheus." A booming growl ripped through the room, and I flung them both into the shimmering darkness, where the pitch black liquid of the portal consumed their bodies.

A prick to my neck caused me to shout, and I dropped my hold on my father. Behind me, hands gripped onto my arms to steady my faltering body. I didn't know who held me or used a drug on me. All I knew was I needed to finish the spell before all my powers became mute. The intoxication of what flowed through me slowly spread, and I was running out of time.

With the remaining breath of power I still held, I whispered, *"I command–thee closed."*

With a single snap of my fingers, a shudder ran through the house as the portal engulfed itself, disappearing completely. I stumbled further backward into the male who gripped me tightly.

His breath whispered across my neck, "I have you, little storm."

I recognized whose voice it belonged to and spat out, "Fuck you, you piece of shit."

Father immediately crowded my face, his hand encased around my throat, squeezing lightly as if to scare but not hurt me.

Seething with anger, his face turned red, and he loudly roared at my lazy, smug smile I aimed at him.

"KOJAX GET IN HERE," his yell ricocheted through the living room, leaving a ringing to buzz within my ears.

When a male named Kojax entered the home, my father let go of my throat and stepped away from me to speak to the new male.

"I need you to gather a few males, jump over to the human realm, and collect my mate unharmed. I don't think I need to put more of an emphasis on the unharmed, do I? Oh, and kill Kalpheus, who is likely to be with her."

"Yes, sir." The male, Kojax, answered, then left the room through the front door and onto the porch. I could hear his muffled instructions through the now-closed door.

I turned my attention and glared at my father. The hate was multiplying, and I was irate at the situation I had gotten myself into.

At least my mother and Kal were safe back in her world. I did wonder how long it would take the males to figure out they couldn't jump to that realm now.

My laughter was soft at first and then transformed into a maniacal cackle. The assassins wouldn't be able to shadow-jump anywhere near Earth, and I would make sure they never would.

Zynas turned my body around and gazed into my eyes with suspicion in his voice. He addressed me, "Little storm, whatever is so funny?"

"You'll see," I whispered. My eyes began to droop from so much exertion. Zynas was practically holding up my body for me. But I was trying to stand on my own. No longer did I want his hands on me. "Get. Your. Hands. Off. Me." I seethed; his touch felt like I was on fire, yet it also lulled me into a sense of safety.

He chuckled, clearly amused at my fiery attitude, "If I let you go, little storm, you will crumple to the floor. And we can't have that. What kind of male would I be if I let my intended fall?"

"I will never be yours. I will fight you when I'm strong enough." I weakly taunted.

"No doubt you will. Your will is as strong as a hurricane. But you will be mine, and I will be yours." He said.

I stared at him while the wheels began to turn in my head. Kal said the same thing to me back on Earth. Had he heard him say it to me? No, that wasn't right. There was no way he could have known what Kal told me in our private moments.

I gave him a vulgar gesture, which only made him laugh harder. Until he straightened himself and dropped the smile, my father turned toward us in the living room with a grin.

"Well, I'm happy to see you two are making up for lost time. We have a lot of our own catching up to do, Raine. I'm eager to reconnect with my daughter. While I am not happy, you have taken away the opportunity for us to be a family by sending your mother away. I am, however, confident my males will be successful. Kojax is a smart male, and he has never let me down. I believe he will prove to be fruitful."

"Speak of the devil," I snickered, eyeing the male my father had just spoken highly of.

In walked a grim-faced Kojax. His eyes took me in for a moment. Pure awe shone before they turned to Zynas and then to my father. "Sir, we have a problem."

My father responded irritably, "What is the issue, Kojax? I would've presumed you and your males would have left by now."

"Yes, that is the hindrance. We were ready to jump, but when we attempted to," The assassin's eyes trained on me again. "It seems your daughter found a way to prevent us from going to the human realm. We have tried several times. We can successfully jump anywhere else but to Earth."

Father turned his attention to me while I continued with the effort to keep my eyes open. Slowly, he walked up, stopping when Zynas let out a growl. "There is more to you than I imagined, isn't there, my little Ashix? You are stronger than I could have dreamed. First, you showed me you could shadow-jump, which I am quite pleased about, and now I find out you have also closed the portals to your mother's home world. I wonder, could you open new ones to new realms we haven't explored yet?" He gripped my cheeks, squeezing them together. "Answer me, my dear."

I attempted to talk through my pinched lips, "I don't know. I have only opened a portal a few times now."

"Don't worry, we will figure that out soon enough. However, we must solve the little problem of you potentially running from us with your new abilities."

He snapped his fingers, and another male jumped into the room next to him, handing over an obsidian silk bag. Digging into the satchel, he produced two beautifully adorned silver bangles. Lifting them to my eyes so I could get a glimpse, he smirked dissolutely.

"These should do. I will have to ask the witch if they will hold against your jumping, but they will ensure you don't use those other powers on anyone else. You will need to earn your freedom, little Ashix. And I'm afraid that won't be for a very long time. Or whenever Zynas decides, he now holds your future."

My father was walking over at an agonizingly slow pace, like I was in a torture chamber, and he was my warden. Looking down at his hands, he gripped the bangles, and I fought Zynas' hold, trying hard to flee the inevitable. "No, no, no. Please don't, PLEASE!" I screamed. The click was deafening as he shut the bangles over each of my wrists.

Gasping, I immediately felt my remaining powers drain into my beautiful prison chains. An uncontrollable sob escaped, and the tears flowed from my eyes as a waterfall river fell over its ledge.

Zy gripped onto my body as I let myself slump. "I hate you–I fucking hate you."

"I know, my storm. You can hate me all you want, but this is for your own good."

"Fuck you, you're a coward who can't even stand up to a female. Are you too afraid I'm going to kick your ass?"

He didn't say another word as he scooped my body up from the ground. I didn't fight. The exhaustion was too much, and the little remaining power I possessed left a space in the void of my body. It had been the catalyst for keeping me from going under.

I lost so much today: my mother, who thankfully was out of my father's clutches. That was more of a win, but I was again separated from her. Kal, whom I was glad I could spare his life for mine. I confessed my love for him, hoping he was okay and wouldn't be too mad at me. My powers were again ripped from me, but I discovered I could shadow-jump.

Ever since I was a little girl, I had dreamed of becoming like the female Shadow Assassins one day. Stronger than the males and more deadlier with just a single look. Now I knew I was more lethal than my male counterparts with my powers mixed in. My wind and lightning, I must have inherited from my mother, while my shadow abilities came from my father. But those powers were no more until I figured out how to get out of my prison. The bangles were beautiful at least, with the same swirling flames that adorned my locket I left back in the human realm, but it shot a pang of homesickness that I might never return to Earth, to family, and to the male I loved, Kal.

The darkness edged my vision when I heard Zy's whispered voice next to my ear, "Sleep, my storm. Everything will be better in time. Just wait."

Chapter Nineteen
Kal

CURSE THE FUCKING GODS! I couldn't believe that Raine would do that to her mother and toss us into the portal like we were fucking rag dolls.

I would ring her beautiful little neck when we got her back. And then I would fuck her until she could no longer walk.

Mmm, yes, that was a great plan. Get her ass back here, spank her, and then fuck her for days, maybe even weeks, making sure she couldn't leave my bed without me carrying her around.

Raine's mother, Pandora, brought me out of my dirty thoughts as she crumpled to the floor in distress. I gingerly walked over to the female who would be my future mother. At that moment, I thought about what I would do if it were my mother and acted on instinct. Gathering her up into my arms, I hugged her tightly. She held me firmly back as she sobbed into my shoulder.

"Don't worry, Pandora, we will rescue her. We'll get her back once I'm strong enough and ask for more help."

"Kalpheus, you need to know something. I won't be able to help open the portal. I died the day the assassins came for Raine. The healers brought me back, but it didn't bring back my powers. I didn't tell Lazarus; I let him believe I still had them. I didn't know what he would do to me if they were gone. I always believed he only thought he loved me, but deep down, I think he just loved the idea of having someone with powers as a mate." She sniffled, and distress crossed her features as she confessed.

"I'm so sorry, Pandora. Everything will be okay. We will figure this out, and we can go to the Hacketts to seek their help."

"Marcus Hackett?" She asked, wiping the wetness from her cheeks.

I huffed, "Well, not Marcus because he's an asshole and doesn't like shadow-jumpers, so he would be no help anyway. No, we will ask his son, Theo, and maybe your best friend, Maggie. She asked about seeing you when you got back. It might be good for you to visit her until we come up with something. I still don't know how long until my full strength and shadow-jumping return."

She nodded, agreeing with what I said as if Maggie had all the answers, "Yes, I suppose I can call her. But after I see my mother and sister, do you know where they are?"

"Last I remember before Raine and I left, they were on a cruise for vacation. I believe they are not set to return for another few weeks."

The front door burst open just then, and the strong scent of lavender and honey filled the room. "RAINE! KALPHEUS!" shouted Samara.

She halted in the doorway and turned pale when she spotted her sister still in my arms. I stood us up and let

Pandora go. Sobs rang out as the two sisters collided, embracing each other.

"Pandi? Is it really you? Holy shit, I can't believe it. Kalpheus, you and Raine did it. You brought her home to us. MOM, GET IN HERE!"

Raine's grandmother, Gigi, walked in and covered her mouth as a gasp escaped. All three females hugged and pushed their foreheads together as if they connected on another level entirely.

Gigi pulled back, gripping Pandora's face and examining deep within her soul, "You have been through hell and back, my girl. I'm so sorry."

"It's okay, Mom. I think if I get close to one of the falls again, it might come back. That's what the legends say, but I don't know for certain," Pandora said.

Samara was looking around the room, and her gaze found mine. "Where's Raine?"

Brushing a hand through my hair, I took a deep breath. I would have to inform these two females that Raine hadn't returned and that she had sacrificed herself to save us. It was difficult to start because all I could think of were those last words she said to me. Raine had told me she loved me, but I hadn't had enough time to say it back to her. She didn't give me that time, and it made me furious. But she loved me, and I held onto that to get me through the process of returning to her.

"She threw us into the portal and then closed it behind her. I think she didn't believe she had enough in her to hold her father back and escape with us. I witnessed him inch closer to her right before. She also shadow-jumped for the first time today, and it was breathtaking. I wish she had come back with us."

"It's alright, Kalpheus, she must have known what she

was doing," Pandora said, trying to make the disastrous situation feel less daunting.

"I hope so, Pandora."

Just then, a male shadow-jumped into the living room, and I didn't stop to assess who it was. I reacted on instinct and tackled the male to the ground. I started choking him, but realized it was Cassius, immediately letting go of his throat. "Cassius?" I said, stunned to see him. I thought he was still in AshFiera, trying to figure out a way to save Pandora.

"Nice to see you, too, asshole." He choked out.

"Sorry, you have no idea the fucked up day we have had," I said, pointing over to Pandora.

His eyes widened as he ran over to her; he scooped Pandora up in a big hug, twirling her around, eliciting the female's laughter.

"Hi, Cassius, it's so good to see you again."

"And I, you, Panda." She blushed at the nickname. Was there something between the two? Raine never mentioned her mother and Cassius being together, but it wasn't my business, and I would stay the hell out of it.

"How in the world are you here? We thought you were back in AshFiera, figuring out how to rescue Pandora from Lazarus." I said.

"Well, I was, but then we got word that something huge was happening when a few dozen Shadow Assassins jumped simultaneously. I stopped by your place to find you, but you weren't there. I followed your shadows, which was fucking hard, by the way, since they have been muted. And well, I could scent Raine here along with her kin's scents. Figured it was safe to jump inside when I heard your voice."

Cassius looked around, but his smile faltered and dropped when his eyes landed back on Pandora. "She's not here, Cass; he has her," Raine's mother said as her bottom lip wobbled.

"Fuck. And Raine has her powers back." Cassius said, remembering what happened at my home when she had touched the locket.

"She does for now. If I know Lazarus, he has already shackled her the same way he imprisoned me. Although he didn't know my powers were completely gone, for the moment." Cass gave her a look, "I'll explain everything later."

Gigi interrupted the reunion to announce that she was going into the kitchen to make tea and grab snacks. She asked me and Samara to accompany her. I assumed she wanted to give Pandora and Cassius time to catch up. She would have to explain to him that the portal was closed, and we wouldn't be getting back the old-fashioned shadow-jumper way.

Walking into the kitchen, I sat on a stool, looking over the counter at all the work Raine had done there. It wasn't trashed like the rest of the house, but she cleaned it anyway. A cookie jar caught my eye; it was out of place, unlike the other jars that were neatly lined along the wall on the counter. Standing from the stool, I approached the out-of-place jar near the stove. Spotting an envelope tucked under the jar, I picked it up, and on the front, written in ink were Gigi and Samara's names.

Turning, I handed the letter to Samara. "I think this is from Raine. She mentioned before we left through the portal that she needed to write you both a letter in case you came home before we returned. I'm not sure what she wrote, but–here." I handed it over so she could read the contents.

Samara ripped it open and began reading it. She was

silent at first, but then returned to the top and read it aloud for Gigi and me to hear.

Dear Gigi and Aunt Samara,

Thank you so much for taking me in, giving me a place to stay, and never asking for anything in return, as well as for introducing me to the Moonbright Club. I have made wonderful friends over the last few months and will miss them dearly. Most of all, I will miss you both with everything I have. I am afraid that if you are reading this, my plans have gone to shit, and I've had to take drastic action. What that dramatic thing is, well, I'm guessing I didn't make it back with Mom and Kal. And that I was left to my own devices to distract my father. I hope Kal and Mom returned safely and are not too mad at me. The most important thing is that they are safe. Please take care of each other.

I love you so much.

P.S. There is another letter behind this one. Please ensure that you give it to Kal on my behalf.

Always, Raine

Samara handed me the following letter. It was still folded, telling me what was within remained untouched. Samara stared at me patiently waiting to hear what mine contained.

Pandora and Cassius walked in just then, and I began unfolding my letter from Raine, but stopped to let Samara reread her letter to them.

"She knew. How could she not have known what she was going to do?" Pandora sobbed. Cassius was right next to her, rubbing her back in comfort. It made my heart ache, and I longed for Raine watching the two of them together.

"Kal, go on, open the letter." Samara encouraged.

Opening the letter, I quickly scanned through it, making sure it didn't contain anything that would embarrass

Raine and me in front of her family. I began to read it out loud;

Dear Kal,

First, I want to tell you how glad I am that you decided to take the stalker job. You have forever altered my life. In the movies on Earth, they ask, 'What is a soulmate?' To me, a soulmate is someone who gets you and loves you for all the flaws within oneself. You, Kalpheus, are my soulmate. I love you and will continue to love you until my last breath. You are mine, and I am yours, forever. Please don't be too mad at what I possibly had to do. I wouldn't change anything and would do it all over again if it meant you and Mom were safe. If you are determined to rescue me, go to the Hacketts. Theo said he memorized my family's ancestral book and would help if we needed it. It might take some time and energy because the original spell Mom used will be rendered unusable when I get to it. Don't worry, though. I'll work my magic on this end. Pissing off any males that I can, kicking ass, and taking names. Until we meet again, because you bet your hunky sexy ass, we will see each other once more.

With all my love,

Raine

Folding the letter, I looked up at the four faces in front of me. They all had somber looks, but Samara was smiling. Giving her a questioning look, she shrugged and added, "She loves antagonizing men. Gage would always tell me how many of the guys at the club would get so flustered because she was relentless. She did it in jest, and they would secretly love it. I have no doubt she will make those men or–males' lives miserable."

She certainly would. Glancing at Gigi, I said the only thing I could muster, "Call the Hacketts. We need to speak with Theo and Maggie."

Chapter Twenty
Raine

B irds were chirping loudly. I swore they were directly in my ear, and it was pissing me off.

I just need five more minutes. Maybe Kal is still in bed with me and will shoo them away.

So I reached over, feeling around the bed. It was empty, aside from some crumpled blankets.

Opening my eyes, I realized I was not in Kal's bed or mine. Then, the past events caught up with me. I was in AshFiera, and apparently, I was in my new room in the mansion that resided in Ozryn.

My father locked me away in a tower like a princess being locked away by a villainous monster. I was by no means a princess, but he was that monster. Everything he did had a nefarious background; no love was involved.

There was a light knock on the door, and a young female walked in with a tray. She was paying attention to what she held, and I assumed she was concentrating on not dropping it. She was shaking when she put it on a small table on the other side of the room from my bed.

"Thank you," I said. The female squeaked, telling me I had startled her.

"I-I'm so sorry, miss. I didn't mean to wake you. P-please don't tell Lord Lazarus." She stammered, shivering in fear.

My eyebrows raised high. What in the world did I get brought back into? From what I remember, there were no titles in AshFiera. Smiling lightly, I tried easing her worries. "Don't worry, Miss?"

"Astora, miss." And she even fucking curtsied.

"Astora, there are no formalities here. You can call me Raine. If my father instructed you to call me by a title, you ignore it, got it?" She nodded her head. "Good, and as far as Lord Lazaraus, he can fuck off. I will neither have you afraid of me nor worried that I will run off to him and tattle like a child. I'm sure you don't know this, but I am not here willingly."

"I didn't know that. T-thank you for being kind. Aside from arriving yesterday, it's my first day here, and I was so nervous about being your maid and whatever else you would require of me." She fidgeted with the hem of her shirt, a sign that she sure was anxious about being near me, or maybe it was being in this place.

"My maid? No, no, I don't need one of those. I will pick up after myself, and if I need anything else, I will retrieve it. When you come here, you can hang out. I have never had a girlfriend before. Back in the human realm, I had a bunch of guys as friends that I would occasionally beat the shit out of." I shrugged as if it were just another Tuesday.

She gasped at my declaration, "Miss-er, Raine, you did all of that? Wow, that is so amazing. I am incredibly envious of you. I don't have any friends, so I would like that very much." It was saddening, and now she was stuck being told to take care of my needs. I wouldn't have that. I needed to know more about my newfound friend.

"So, Astora, what in the world made you want to get this gig?"

She hummed before answering, "Well, I didn't want the job. My father is a Shadow Assassin and owes Lord Lazarus a favor. When they brought you in, you were unconscious. I was already here waiting for your arrival."

"Fuck me, so you are a hostage as well. Those bastard males. Well, don't worry, we girls have to stick together, alright?"

Astora grinned widely and then started tidying around the room. "Hey, didn't I say none of that?" I chastised her.

"Sorry, Raine. It's a nervous habit. I need to clean or organize stuff. I know you said I had nothing to worry about, but it helps."

"Well, come sit down at the table with me when you are ready. I would like to have breakfast with a companion. There is so much food on this tray. And there's absolutely no way I'm going to finish it all myself."

She inclined her head and continued to move items ever so slightly around. I left her to it, getting out of bed. I needed to pee so bad my bladder started hurting.

Doing my business quickly, I walked over to the sink and washed my hands. Staring at myself in the mirror, I took in the dark circles under my eyes, indicating I exerted too much yesterday and didn't get enough rest. My hair was a disaster. Waves stuck out everywhere, so I ran my fingers through my hair to tame it slightly. As my hands were in the strands, the new jewelry my father gifted me caught my attention.

Examining my wrists, I fingered each bangle. They were beautiful.

I would give my father that much credit. However, they were the bane of my existence since they muted my powers along with the drug that was still coursing through my body.

It would be days, possibly weeks, before I could feel any inclination of power, if at all.

Dropping my hands, I walked out to the table where the food was. Astora was already sitting with a plate filled and happily munching away. I smiled, grateful I now had a new friend in this prison. She would keep me sane, at least.

We sat together in silence, filling our bellies full. Astora had to leave shortly after breakfast, though. Father had more work she was required to do, and she wanted to finish before lunch was served.

I was alone with my thoughts for hours. Walking circles in my new bedroom, I took in all the details. The furniture and pictures hanging on the walls were filled with decorative Ashix; it would be almost obnoxious to anyone else who didn't love the beasts, but I thought they were perfect.

Thinking of Beauty, I spotted a globe filled with water and glitter next to my bed. In the center, sitting on a boulder, was a replica of my Ashix. It was identical to her, even down to the coloring of her scales and eyes. The stunning shimmer of her pearlescent scales and angry, burnt-orange orbs brought tears to my eyes.

Did my father get this made for me to torture me? He knew how much Beauty meant. Which only left me with more questions when I thought of her disappearance again. Did he have something to do with it? Did he kill her? Was she even free, or was she shackled just like I was?

Walking over to the window with the globe still in my hand, I spotted a bench against it. Letting whoever sat here watch the outside world. I brushed my fingers against the pillows I would use as a backrest and sat down.

My bedroom was high above the ground, no doubt designed so I wouldn't try to escape from the window. It left me high enough to view all sorts of people walking around, doing their business with zero clue I was up here.

Leaning against the window, I breathed in slowly and then released it steadily outward. A thump resounded in my bedroom, causing me to snap my head in the direction it came from.

Zynas was standing in the middle of my room. His body decked out in his assassin get-up. A tight black t-shirt showcased his impressive flat abs, which were also accentuated by several straps crisscrossing over his chest. They held several small daggers along with a few syringes. Those must have contained the shit he injected me with. My gaze traveled down to his black cargo pants and black combat boots. I lifted my eyes back up to his face. He smirked, lifting one side of his lips, revealing an enticing fang. It made my heart jump.

Why in the world did my body react to this male? Staring at the eye patch next, a little longer than I should have, I was suddenly curious about why he was wearing one. The first time I met Zynas, he had both eyes. I noticed his hair was shorter as I watched him run a gloved hand through it.

"What happened to your eye? The first time we met, you had both of them." I asked, abruptly, not caring for how rude it sounded out loud.

He froze, and his smile dropped. "Your father took it."

"Wh-What?!"

"You heard me, Raine. I said he took it." He repeated.

"So he took your eye, and you're still helping him? Wow, you are more fucked up than I realized." I pointed out, crossing my arms to hold myself back from reaching out for him. To what? Comfort him because of something my father had done?

"You have no idea what you are talking about." He sneered.

"Unless you tell me what happened, then I will never know, now will I?"

"Maybe another time, little storm. Your father is waiting for us."

"Waiting for us where? I don't want to go anywhere with you or see him, for that matter." I said, stomping my foot down.

"Don't act like a child, Raine. Let's go. You'll want to see what he has for you."

That caught my attention. I didn't ask what my father had because I knew the asshole wouldn't tell me anyway. I placed the globe back on my bedside table and headed for the door in front of Zynas. Before I could walk past, he wrapped an arm around my waist.

"What do you think you are doing? Get, shoo, don't touch."

Clenching his jaw together, he didn't say a word, holding on tighter to my side. We disappeared from my room and into a large ballroom, where several males were waiting.

I looked up at Zynas and hissed, "You could have fucking said you were going to jump with me, dick head."

He grunted, keeping his hand on my lower back, guiding me ahead. He was looking at my father, standing in the middle of the large, empty ballroom. My father's smile widened when he gazed at where Zynas had his hand. So, I attempted to step aside to lose contact. But Zy was too quick, and he gripped the back of my shirt. A low, barely audible growl escaped him, and I stopped my movements.

"My little Ashix, I am so glad you could join us. I wish to speak to you about what will be expected of you once you've settled in." It was as if my father had slapped me across the face himself as I reared back.

"Expected of me? Really? Am I not a prisoner, Father?" I said, holding out my wrists to him, flashing the jewelry he so aptly put on me.

"No, Raine. I wish for us to be a family and for you to have your freedom. Within reason, of course. I'm hoping you will get over this childish tantrum and hatred for your dear old dad over time."

Rolling my eyes, I uttered angrily, "Gonna be a very long time before that happens."

"Yes, I have a surprise for you that I hope will change your mind."

"And what is that-"

Several shadow-jumpers appeared, along with a large, angry beast. Not just any beast but my Ashix– "Beauty!" I screamed, starting to run toward her, but I was abruptly stopped as Zy jumped in front of my body. "Move, you big fucking idiot," I said through clenched teeth.

The roaring intensified, shaking the floor underneath my feet. Beauty heard my voice and spotted Zynas blocking my attempts to reach her. She was striving to break free so she could get to me. And my heart was shattering watching her struggle. They had her chained up and a muzzle over her mouth, which I guessed was to prevent her from using her fires.

"Let me get to her, please. She's going to hurt herself. Please!" I pleaded into the room to anyone who would listen.

Zy moved to the side, and I bolted the rest of the way to her. She saw me coming and instantly settled down. When

I reached her, I placed my forehead on her, closing my eyes, and I rubbed a hand along her long neck, whispering low, "I'm here, girl. Goddess, I missed you so much."

Pulling back, I looked into her deep, burnt orange eyes and felt something click inside my mind. Her rush of emotions invaded, flowing as easily as water. They were glorious and confusing. Her hatred for the males surrounding us was loud, but her love for me was over-powering.

A cry left my throat, causing me to grip her muzzle, while I fell to my knees. Dragging her face down with me in the process. "I'm sorry." I wept. She responded by gripping me in her shackled claws, tucking me close to her body and under her long neck in protection.

A growl echoed into the room, and I felt her head snap up, ready to attack. My father's voice carried across the room toward us, but I couldn't understand what he was saying. Father didn't dare come close to Beauty when she was aggressive, so Zy was the only male I knew who would dare do such a thing. Glancing over my shoulder, I saw his hands up placatingly, which only made me snort.

"She doesn't like males, you know. I wouldn't come any closer unless you want to lose a hand along with that missing eye."

"I only want to make sure you are alright. You screamed, but I see now that you are not injured." His concern was unwarranted and unwanted. As if he genuinely cared.

"You think Beauty would hurt me? Never–she is my first friend. She thinks you are coming to take me away."

"Your father wants to finish the conversation." He said curtly.

I nodded, understanding that this was a brief visit, if

only momentarily, "Give me a second." Standing, I wrapped my arms around Beauty's neck. "Don't worry, girl. I'll figure out a way to get back to you. Now that I know you are here, nothing will stop me, I swear. I love you, Beauty."

The burst of affection in my head was all the answer I needed. Glaring at Zynas, she huffed a puff of smoke in his direction, and I laughed loudly. "Good girl," I said, patting her neck. And then, hesitantly, I walked away back toward my father.

It was a dreadful walk. My father saw how I reacted when I was reunited with her. He would use that to his advantage, and my weakness was that I would agree to his terms. Dragging my feet, I glanced up at the male I so despised. "What do you want?"

He grinned, the smile menacing like a psychopath, and said, "I want you to behave. Listen to my instructions and Zynas's. But most of all, I want you to be my daughter and treat me like I am your father."

Cocking an eyebrow, suspicion rolled through me, so I asked, "That's all you want from me?"

"Mhm, for the most part. There might be other things, but I am sure you will be more agreeable with time." He crooned.

Looking over at where Zynas was standing, he gave me a tentative smile and nodded. His gaze softened the longer I peered at him, and it made me uncomfortable. Turning away, I returned my attention to my father.

"I will agree to your terms on the condition that I get unlimited access to Beauty. You took her from me, and I will not be without my Ashix anymore. Remember what mother said? I am connected to her, a blessing from the Goddess herself."

He paused, drawing out the anticipation. I needed him

to agree. This new connection that formed with Beauty needed to be explored. For some reason, it triggered when I came back to AshFiera. Even with my powers muted, I needed to understand why.

"Alright, my little Ashix. You can have unlimited access to the beast. But, either Zynas or one of my other males must accompany you while you visit with her." He said.

Shit, it would have to do, though. There was no other way around it, and I needed to take advantage of his generosity while it was available.

"Thank you, Father," I said, and he beamed, knowing he was getting his way for now.

Zy stepped up beside me, wrapping his arm around my waist again. "We should be off, sir. I would like to speak with Raine in private. May we have your leave?"

Father grunted his agreement and disappeared, jumping out of the ballroom. I went to open my mouth when Zy placed his finger against my lips. "Not here. Let me take us back to your room." I inclined my head and held onto his hand that gripped my side.

Back in my room, I stepped away from him immediately, and he dropped his hand to resume at his side. He walked up to the window I had been peering out of earlier and looked out. Facing away from me, he spoke, "When you decide to visit your beast, I will be the only one to take you. No other male will be allowed to be alone with you."

I glared at the back of his head, furious that he thought to order me around, "And you're the boss of me?"

"Yes, I am your betrothed."

"I won't mate you. I am with Kal. I love him." I said, hoping to hurt him and dig an invisible dagger through his beating heart.

He didn't flinch like I thought he would, "Doesn't

matter," He lowered his voice, "I will fit him into the equation. But you are mine."

"What do you mean–fit him into the equation? He's back in the human realm, and I'm captive here. There's something I'm missing."

He chose not to say another word and disappeared.

What the actual fuck did he mean? Why are there always more questions than answers with him?

Frustrated, I perched myself on the bench, rubbing my beautiful shackles and looking back out across the bustling city, as this was now my view for the foreseeable future.

Chapter Twenty-One
Zynas

What an infuriating female. I wanted to give her a piece of my mind and make her see the bigger picture. She made me want to tell her everything, but I still had eyes and ears on my movements. I was never truly alone aside from my thoughts. But those turned dark most of the time, and I hated being with myself. So, I would deal with the constant monitoring.

For the next few weeks, I was determined to prove to her father, Lazarus, that I was a trustworthy male and successfully convince Raine to behave. Then he would relax the security, but until that happened, I needed to be careful about what I said to her, and I nearly slipped up in her bedroom today.

Thankfully, when my father was still alive, he had that room spelled by a witch from the human realm. It was his sanctuary, where he would meet with others to discuss private matters of great importance.

Thinking of my father, I reminded myself that the bastard took my father's life along with my left eye.

It was a shame, the eye.

It made things trickier but not impossible. I wasn't at a considerable loss without it. I adapted quickly once it was gone.

My father's death, though, I would seek my vengeance against 'Lord Lazarus' one day.

What a joke. Did he think this was his kingdom? Stealing my home for himself and creating chaos within the shadow ranks. When most shadow-jumpers craved order, obedience, and loyalty. The organization was mine. I trained my entire life to take over for my father. To keep order.

Lazarus was the opposite of it all.

I needed to find my most trusted male and pass an encrypted letter to him. Only he could decipher the words and report to the other males we both trusted. They needed to know that the self-proclaimed lord had Raine's Ashix, which would complicate matters.

She always had a soft spot for animals. It was clear to see the day I met her and lost her all at once.

But I had watched her from afar without the beast spotting me. Some days were more challenging than others since she liked to patrol around the home before perching atop that gods damn boulder. I quickly learned her routine and stayed out of the way most days.

"Zynas!" Shouted one of the males near the stables, where the Ashix was housed. "Zynas, we need your help. Get over here." An ear-piercing roar sounded from the building, and I swore under my breath.

It seemed Beauty was throwing a fit without her companion. I would need to go into the stables and attempt to calm her. Although it appeared she didn't like me, I wasn't afraid of her. I was confident I would win her over soon. I had to see if I could get her free. My little storm would refuse to flee when it came time until we rescued the beast. So, I would make things easier by letting the ferocious beast see I wasn't a threat. Any trust, she would allow me; I needed to seize it.

I entered the stables just in time to see a male trying to finish securing her chains, when she threw him into the wall.

I gripped the chains and tugged, "Beauty!" She turned toward my deep, booming voice and snarled. "It seems you remember me, don't you, female?" She huffed a puff of smoke out the sides of the muzzle in answer. "Calm, and I will bring Raine to see you soon."

That had her attention. She hesitantly laid on her stomach, giving me more slack on the chains. Keeping an eye on my movements, I latched the remaining chain and backed away slowly.

"It's for your own good, Beauty. If you remain calm, some of these chains might lessen. The amount we have to tie you down with is overkill, but no one wants to end up dead."

She canted her head like a dog did when you spoke with an excited-pitched voice, but she seemed to understand what I was telling her.

Walking closer to the Ashix, I held out my hand, palm up towards her flaring nostrils, letting her smell that I wasn't a threat. She sniffed a few times while keeping her eyes trained on mine. I smiled when she sat up, huffing without the smoke billowing out.

It was progress, faster than I thought I would make today.

"Wow, you have a way with the beast, Zynas. Maybe you could help around the stables."

Glaring at the male, he shrank into himself, muttered an

apology, and ran off. I was alone with the Ashix, so I pulled up a chair to sit with her. She eyed me wearily but turned her head when she decided I wasn't going to hurt her, and closed her eyes to rest.

Speaking softly to my soon-to-be-mate's bonded animal, I reassured her, "Don't worry, Beauty. I'm going to take care of you and my little storm."

A Note From The Author

Hey Reader! You're probably never going to read this, but for those who do, this is the second edition of my debut. If you're writing a book for the first time, learn from me and... Read. It. Out. Loud. No, seriously, make sure you read it out loud after your first round of edits and do it every single time you go back through and do those edits, whether it's once or ten times. This took me six months to edit after I decided it needed some major revisions, and that was after I had written two more books. Look, we all make mistakes, and that's totally okay. It allowed me to create fun chapter headers and ornamental breaks for this book. Plus, who doesn't love a little extra pazzazz with their books?

Anyway, thank you so much for reading my debut, and I hope you continue to dive into further books I have written, because let's be for real, I'm going to have MANY more! There are way too many stories untold swirling in my brain and in the many notebooks I have hoarded from the dollar store.

Happy reading, AnderSinners, kisses XOXO!

About the Author

K.L. ANDERSEN is a multi-genre romance author and avid reader. Whether it's heart-wrenching or silly, she likes to write and dream up different worlds and the not-so-human men in them. She is a fierce Scorpio who lives in the Northern Midwest with her husband, two kids, two dogs, two cats, a bearded dragon, and the many chickens who roam around her home.

You can find her being a goober while enjoying writing, reading, gaming, or hanging out with those she loves.

Books by K.L. Andersen

An AshFieran Duet

AshFiera

Ashix Rising

Mount Hellfire Mates

Infernal Hearts

www.ingramcontent.com/pod-product-compliance
Lightning Source LLC
Chambersburg PA
CBHW070052260626
47160CB00004B/1184